AND THE WOLVES WILL HOWL AT THE BLOODMOON

Book Three Of The BloodMoon Trilogy

Mercy Ashes

Mercy Ashes

To Shirley
always be the
Phoenix in your
own story and
rise from the ashes
Mercy
Ashes
♡

CONTENTS

BLURB –

A person from Ember's past appears, but how much of a threat are they really? Join Ember on her journey into adulthood, and eventually into Motherhood as she finally gets justice against Jameson and gets the calm life she's always wanted, well, as calm as pack life can be when you are the pack Luna with ten mates.

TRIGGER WARNINGS:

This series contains triggers that include:

Threat of child rape.
Child molesting.
Child torture.
Child abuse.
Child neglect.
Death of a baby.
** Murder/Manslaughter
Child Abandonment.
A child is being forced to take drugs.
There are some references to trafficking.
Bloodplay (during FMC period)
Suicidal thoughts of a minor (FMC)
Suicide attempts by a minor (FMC)
OOT Protective Alpha & Pack mates (harem)
OOT Protective Luna
Oral rape of a minor (MMC)

Also, because this series takes place in a supernatural setting, there are references to age gap fated mates.

There are fewer of these in books two and three, with them only being references to the past.

There is MM within the Harem between two members, including group scenes. The FMC's twin is also gay and has his own harem

TimeLine

BIRTH: 31ST DECEMBER

Group Home

4 YEARS OLD

BLOODWOLF PACK 14TH MARCH

6 YEARS OLD

HELLBLOOD MOTORCYCLE CLUB 3RD JANUARY

7 YEARS OLD

GROUP HOME 12TH JANUARY
TWIN TREES PACK 2ND FEBUARY
GROUP HOME 18TH APRIL
THE DEN 1ST MAY
GROUP HOME 25TH DECEMBER

8 YEARS OLD

SHARPE FAMILY 10TH JAUARY
CLAWFANG PACK 15TH MAY
GROUP HOME 6TH AUGUST
LANE FAMILY 23RD NOVEMBER

9 YEARS OLD

ARMATIGE FAMILY 22ND JANUARY
GROUP HOME 17TH APRIL
TRACY FAMILY 27TH APRIL
QUADRIVER PACK 6TH JULY
JACOBEY FAMILY 10TH OCTOBER
LAKEVIEW PACK 6TH NOVEMBER

10 YEARS OLD

THE TANK 4TH FEBUARY
GROUP HOME 1ST DECEMBER
THE CAGE 17TH DECEMBER

11 YEARS OLD

GROUP HOME 3RD SEPTEMBER
HOSPITAL 15TH SEPTEMBER
THE PIT 17TH SEPTEMBER

12 YEARS OLD,
13 YEARS OLD

HOSPITAL 1ST JULY
SHIELD FAMILY 8TH JULY

14 YEARS OLD
15 YEARS OLD

HALFWAY HOUSE 1ST AUGUST

16 YEARS OLD

LENNOX PACK 4TH NOVEMBER
HOSPITAL MID DECEMBER 2018

17 YEARS OLD

TRIPLE MOON PACK 21ST JANUARY

18 YEARS OLD

BLOODMOON PACK 31ST DECEMBER

THE TRIPLEMOON FAMILY TREE

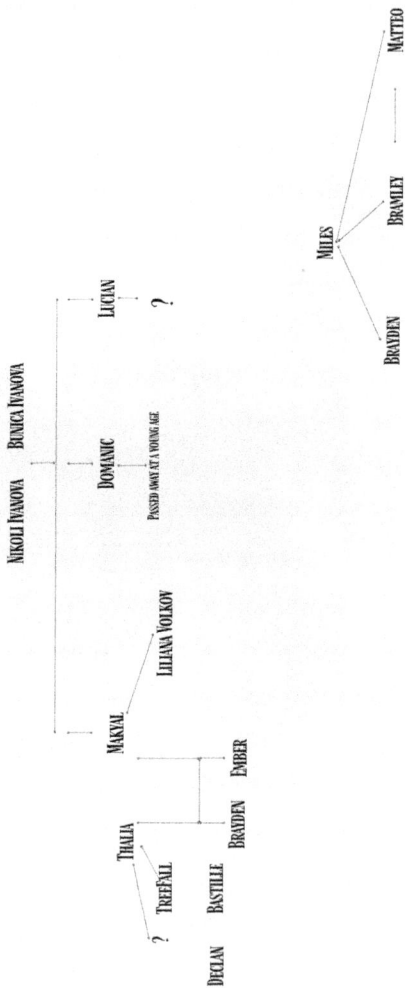

Nikoli Ivanova — **Bunica Ivanova**

Domanic
PASSED AWAY AT A YOUNG AGE

Lucian
?

Makyal — **Liliana Volkov**

Thalia
? — **TreeFall**

Bastille

Brayden

Ember

Declan

Miles

Brayden

Bramley ———

Matteo

THE TREEFALL FAMILY TREE

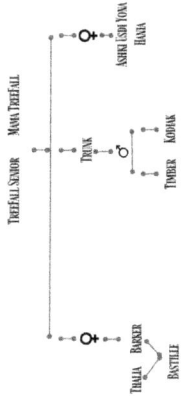

TREEFALL SENIOR   MAMA TREEFALL

THALIA   BARKER

THUNK

ASHEN ASH YONA

BASTILLE

TIMBER   KODIAK

HAVEN

WHO IS WHO

EMBERS MATES

REN FIREFALL - ALPHA WOLF
JENSON FALL - KITSUNE
CREED TATE - INCUBUS/WOLF HYBRID
JACE TATE - WOLF/INCUBUS HYBRID
KODIAK TREEFALL - ALASKAN MOUNTAIN BEAR
DARBY O'CONNERS - DRAGON
DEVIN MOORE - VAMPIRE
SAINT KNIGHT - NIGHTMARE
RIVER KNIGHT - NIGHTMARE
PAYTON STONE - BASILISK

OTHER MAIN CHARACTERS

GIOVANNI MICHAELS - VAMPIRE - SOCIAL WORKER
IGNATIOUS SALVATOR - DRAGON - LAWYER

HELLHOUNDS

POPS - REGINALD
NONNA - PASSED
LAYTON
DECON
BEAR
RACHET
SILAS
LINK
RYLAND, AJAX, CIN (THE LITTER)

RELUCTANTLY ADDED

SAMUAL JAMESON - SOCIAL WORKER - MAGE

FAMILY MEMBERS

MAYHAL IVANOVA - EMBER'S FATHER - ALPHA WOLF
DOMINIC IVANOVA - TRIPLEMOON ALPHA, EMBER'S UNCLE - ALPHA WOLF
LUCIAN IVANOVA - TRIPLEMOON BETA, EMBER'S UNCLE - BETA WOLF
NIKOLI IVANOVA - EMBER'S GRANDFATHER - ALPHA WOLF
DECLAN TREEFALL - TRIPLEMOON'S FUTURE ALPHA, EMBER'S HALF-BROTHER - VAMPIRE
BASTILLE TREEFALL - EMBER'S HALF-BROTHER - ALASKAN MOUNTAIN BEAR
BRAIDEN HYBRIS IVANOVA - EMBER'S TWIN BROTHER - PUOL BETA WOLF

MILES - OMEGA ALBINO PANTHER - BRANDEN'S MATE
BRANKLEY STOKES - DRAGON/VAMPIRE HYBRID - MILES AND MATTEO'S MATE
MATTEO MICHAELS - CRYSTAL MAGE - MILES AND BRANKLEY'S MATE

LILLIANA VOLKOV - SKETCHERS - MAYHAL'S MATE
PRINCE LIAM GIBERSON - VAMPIRE PRINCE
SIR NATHANIEL PRINCE - VAMPIRE - ROYAL GUARD

ALMA GRIMOY - ELEMENTAL MAGE - TRIPLEMOON HOUSEKEEPER

TITIAN TREEFALL - ALASKAN MOUNTAIN BEAR, KODIAK'S GRANDFATHER, BASTILLE'S UNCLE
TIMBER TREEFALL - ALASKAN MOUNTAIN BEAR - KODIAK'S OLDER BROTHER
XANDER FIREFALL - BETA WOLD - REN AND JENSON'S OLDER HALF - BROTHER

PROLOGUE

BRAYDEN

There has never been a time I wanted to be in my best friend's shoes. I have always been happy to be his trainer; at the end of the day, It was my idea. But after hearing the words that were snarked at Ren when he entered the ring. I really want to switch places. This smirking piece of shit, who drugged, tried to rape, and marked my sister's skin, thinks he has a claim on her, but he's about to learn.

I watch and assess the Beta in the ring; he only seems to have defensive moves. Ren could easily take him down with a punch or a roundhouse. But instead, he's playing with him, making it seem like 'Alpha Nox' has a shot at winning this.

I can't hear what the shit stain is saying, and Goddess knows how Ren is keeping Pine under control. Lennox starts to get frustrated and tries to go on the offensive, but its sloppy, 'how the fuck did he win to get here?', Ren is still playing, and deflects it easily, Ren switches to grappling rather than kicks and punches, as the clock ticks to forty-five minutes and he gets Lennox into an arm lock, pinning him to the mat, one sharp jolt and Ren will break Lennox's arm, five minutes Lennox attempts to wiggle out of the hold, spewing shit about my sister, but eventually he taps out.

Ren wins.

I jump into the ring, but right before I get to Ren's side, Lennox goes to attack his back, claws partially shifted, Ren sensing something coming, does a bounce-house kick and knocks the fucker out. Unfortunately, the human ref gets snicked by a claw. Brilliant, I quickly look to Uncle Luc and signal that there may be a problem.

I join Ren as he's handed the newcomer's belt, and on Ember's recommendation, I talk to him, distracting him from the photos so he doesn't tense up.

"Just look at Em, bro, ignore the cameras." Em is bouncing up and down, cheering and yelling insults simultaneously like she did the whole match. I tried not to take my eyes off Lennox, but I had to make sure she was okay.

"Yeah, probably not a good idea. I don't want to pop a boner," he chuckles.

"Yuck, she's my sister," I reply, but yeah, it was not a good idea to get a boner while having photos taken that we had no control over.

We hop out of the ring, and I notice Miles sorting Ember's hair out.

"Lone Wolf" she yells as she hops the barrier, strides to Ren, hooks his neck with her hand and pulls him for a kiss, one hand on his hip, the other now resting on his heart, he has the belt hooked on his forearm while he palms her ass 'come on dude, she's my sister' the other hand is cuffing her throat, I notice a smirking Creed adjust himself between shots then he clears his throat, Ren scowls at him and Ember glancing over her shoulder and smirks at him, Creed winks, Embers way of relaxing Ren and getting the shots they want I guess.

Ren turns and strides off. I then notice Ember's smug look, but I just follow Ren with a shake of my head, 'sisters'. Creed is on our heels, snapping a few more shots,

"Just to let you guys know, Smudge and Miles designed her top, the back has 'Lone Wolfs Luna' printed on it, she was staking her claim to all the thirsty bitches". With that, he turns and heads back to the main room, Ren and I gawping at his back.

CHAPTER ONE

EMBER

Ren and Bray stride off down the corridor towards the locker room, and I hop back over the barrier to join the others. Creed reappears from getting some last shots of Ren Post-match, and thankfully, 'Alpha Nox' has scurried off when the media headed towards them.

"Creed, I need photos for his websites and media pages ASAP." Devin chirps, swiping at some things on his tablet,

"It's okay, babe. They all go straight to my laptop, cleaning up one of our gorgeous Luna, getting her perk ass squeezed right now. Come pick which others you want." Darby snarks with a wink, the guy's joke around and grumble that it wasn't a fair fight.

Miles holds my hand as we people-watch, which is mainly him complaining about how some people are dressed. A group of girls wearing ribbons, as Miles puts it, come to stand in front of our section. Matt's head appears between mine and Miles, kissing his mate's cheek.

"What are they doing?" He asks before I get a chance to give him some sass. Lily twists in front of Miles to look at us,

"They are either trying to get in press photos or grab your boys' attention." She looks at them with disgust,

"They are how succubae get a bad name," she spits the words,

"They are human, Lily, but I understand the reference; they think they can get to Ren and Brayden through you guys." Bram looks confused

"Why? How?" I glance at him as I hear the girls talk about how hot the trainer was, and if he's single, and how my kiss was obviously a publicity stunt, as someone as hot as The Lone Wolf couldn't really be with a fat ginger like that.

"They get into your beds, you brag how amazing they were, so Ren and Bray then pick up your sloppy seconds, they're gold and fame diggers, not that you guys, my twin brother or my Fiancé will fall for any of that," I state loud enough for the rag-wearing girls to hear me.

"They don't expect my twin to have a hot boyfriend, or someone like Ren to be engaged to someone short and dumpy, they believe they will sway the boys with legs that need to be held closed by tight dresses." I stand, and so do Miles and Lily, both giving the girls a finger wave.

The venue security comes over to escort the girls out, and they all loudly protest, saying they are part of our group, but they don't know any of our names. The media department pushes its way to us as we get out of the seating area.

"Miss, can I ask you some questions?" one guy asks while simultaneously sticking a mic and camera in my face,

"No, you may not. Let me introduce you to Devin Moore, 'Lone Wolfs' manager. He can answer any questions you have." Declan and Kodi step between us and them, shielding us from cameras. Once Devin has finished answering questions and ignoring some, we head outside to the cars.

We are nearly at one of the cars when I feel the air shift. I drop my head, realising it's probably the Lennox pack,

"Matt... get Lily and Miles in the car, lock the doors, do not come out for anything and text the guys, Ren is not allowed to come out. The Media would have a field day." I get a grunt from Matt as he pulls Miles and Lily to the car. Once the locks click, Dad comes to my side.

"Stop hiding in the shadows, step forward and state your business."

Dad's alpha command, lacing his words,

"No one shift, appear human, cameras are watching." Nate's words are but a mutter, and I see something out of the corner of my eye and spot the guy from inside, crouching behind a minivan.

CHAPTER TWO

REN

"Matt has just texted me, we need to stay here. Something is kicking off, but the media has eyes on them." Bray says, then looks at me with a sigh,

"I don't like it either, but I trust our family to keep my mate and my sister safe," I nod as he finishes, then his phone rings with a video call.

"Lily is filming, my phone is on mute, so she won't pick up your voices, but I thought you would want to see what's happening." Matt's voice comes through as Miles gives a nervous wave, and then the camera turns to watch out the car window.

My gorgeous mate stands shoulder to shoulder with Declan and Mika, well, kind of. Declan is 6ft 2, Mika is 6ft 4, and my badass mate is 4ft 9, but she's a fighter and a survivor, goddess, I love her, and because she didn't get in the car with the others without me by her side, I'm going to spank her ass red when I get home.

EMBER

Dad's command rings out, but no one moves. I pull my retractable baton from inside my jacket and flick it out.

"Cowards," I mutter, which makes Declan chuckle.

Jericho Lennox storms forward with five guys at his back, all bigger and stronger than he is. One is a weak Alpha, whereas Lennox's name is all the strength he has.

"Where's Firefall?" he sneers, looking around,

"With the press, drinking champagne and celebrating his win." Declan snarks with a chuckle, and I smirk.

"Well, I'll just take his whore, as he will have hotter, less desperate pussy falling at his feet now." He reaches for me, and I bat his hand away.

"Try to touch my daughter again, and you will get more than a slapped wrist," Dad says so calmly that I can see the General peeking through. Two of Lennox's guys go pale and step back, including the Alpha.

"Don't think they realised she was one of us when he tried to drug and rape her dad, but I am curious if there are hotter and better out there, why is he trying so hard to get his hands on her?" Declan says, inspecting his nails, then chuckles as thirty people leave the shadows.

"I don't think my social worker shared my parentage while he tried to keep me hidden," I state, shifting my footing, ready for what is most likely going to happen,

"But Samuel Jameson likes skirting the rule book, so he could really have told them anything," I state clearly enough that the media guy can hear me, he's moved now, so he has a clear shot with his camera of what's happening,

"Well, you come with us like originally planned, You can mate my nephew, and our families can have an alliance." the older, creepy, man walks towards us, his eyes never stop roaming my body as he licks his lips and rubs his hands together, I visibly shudder at the thought of him and step closer to my brother, holding up my left hand,

"Pass, I'm engaged to Ren Firefall." I can hear the nausea in my voice as I hold back bile at the thought of leaving with them.

"Shame, but we did try peacefully, I guess." Alpha Lennox mumbles, then lunges towards me. Dec knocks him away as Dad takes a blow from the side, and Jericho moves towards me.

"Time for us to roll in the dirt again, I can't wait to feel your soft flesh beneath my hands, I've touched myself to the memory countless times, I now need bitches to fight back, or I don't cum hard enough, none fight me as you do though." He tries to sound seductive, but it's just creepy.

"The fact you have to pay or drug girls to have sex with you says a lot, Beta Nox." At my words, he lunges again, and I fall into my training. I don't have Rohypnol running through my veins this time, I don't hit out with the baton, but I do use it to block his hits and knock away his grabs, much like his fight with Ren, he gets pissed and then sloppy.

I hear police sirens, but he keeps coming even as blue lights streak across the parking lot. I smirk, which causes him to falter enough for me to bounce-house kick him. He goes down like a sack of shit. Matt storms from the car with Lily hot on his heels. I see Miles shaking in the car, but Bram is already on his way over, so I stay where I am.

Matt asks the officer closest to me for a number or email address to send the video to. He watches Matt send it and then calls to check that it was received. Lily gives him our address, and after twenty-five minutes of questions, it probably would have been longer if the senior officer hadn't served with Dad after a man hug and plans to catch up, now that Dad has found me, we head home.

I head straight to Ren's room and shower, wanting to get Lennox's touch off me again. It's not as bad this time, but I still feel gross.

Before I reach his closet for a t-shirt, I'm grabbed and thrown on the bed. I only have time to register that there is no foreign scent before words are snarled into my ear.

"Why the fuck didn't you get into the car?" Then a sharp slap hits my ass.

CHAPTER THREE

REN

I spank Ember ten times five on each ass cheek, before thrusting into her. I feel like shit for not checking she was wet for me, but I'm too pissed. I can smell she's turned on, then she lets out a low moan with no pain laced in there, cuffing her nape and pinning her to the bed, I pound into her, my hips slapping against her red ass, my balls swinging so they slap against her clit.

"You make me so fucking mad. Not only did you tell me not to come to protect you, but you just stood there ready to fight." She doesn't try to answer me, but gasps and moans leak from her with each of my thrusts.

"You don't cum until I fucking tell you that you can." I lace my words with command, knowing she can deny it, but I want her to understand, she needs to understand how it made me feel, I cum inside her, my muscles relaxing, and I slow my thrusts, I release her nape, and she pushes up to her hands and knees, pressing back against me, I pull her up against my chest cuffing her throat, I love this position, she's so tiny in front of me, my Alpha side loves to feel that we are dominating our Luna, I tease her dusky nipples with my other hand, she steadies herself by holding my ass cheek and forearm, pulling me against her with each thrust.

"I'm not sorry for protecting your career or defending myself,"
She murmurs against my lips, swallowing my moans as I cum again inside her, her cunt fluttering around me. She's so close, but she isn't allowed yet, so I let my fear of losing her and her getting hurt fill our bond as I kiss her.

EMBER

I know he's angry because he was scared. I also know he's been edging me for the last two hours as punishment, but he needs the connection to reassure himself that I'm okay. He's kissing me like I nearly died, he pulls away, pushing me so I land on my back, I gasp a breath before his cock is pounding into me again, and his mouth is on mine, he cums twice more before he pulls away to speak against my lips,

"Promise we will fight side by side from now on, no more sacrificing ourselves for the other? Promise me, baby! I can't lose you!" Ren begs as he starts to make love to me, slow, deep thrusts, kissing over his bite marks, the way his hips roll is putting much-needed friction against my clit,

"I can't promise that, and neither can you, but I will always promise to have someone at my side if I have to fight. But I will never run." My voice is a whine by the end.

"Please, Alpha, let me cum, I need to cum around your cock, let that be proof I'm here, I'm alive, I'm yours, please, my Alpha." I kiss his jaw, trying to pull his knot inside my desperate pussy,

"Mmmm, cum my Luna, fall apart in my arms," he bites down over my mark, not enough to break the skin, but enough to detonate a series of orgasms. My back arches as his knot slips inside me

"Mind, Body, Heart and Soul, I'm yours for eternity. I love you, my Alpha." I whisper out; my words seem to snap something inside of him, slipping a hand under my ass so my hips are tilted, his cock now hitting that excellent spot inside of me.

"Mind, Body, Heart and Soul, I'm yours for eternity. I love you, my Luna, I love you so much it hurts, baby." Eventually, our lovemaking slows, and like his thrusts, our kisses are slow and deep, his knot is still locking us together, but he takes us to the shower, where I cum twice more, and his knot shrinks enough to free my now sore pussy, once we are clean and dressed, me in a t-shirt, him in a pair of boxers, we climb back into bed holding each other close.

"Two months, Ember, then we are on the countdown to when you fall pregnant then I expect you to run if there is danger, or I will lock you away to keep you and our babies safe", his voice is a sleepy growl, I don't answer, the only time I would run is if I can't win the fight or the risk is too great.

CHAPTER FOUR

EMBER

Ren and I sleep until after 2 pm, or well, I do. I wake Ren with my mouth. I'm already dressed, so I save my very sore parts from another round. Plus, when my tummy protests loudly, I get a grumpy growl and we head down, hoping Alma saved us some lunch. The amazing woman she is, there is plenty of food waiting.

"The police are at the gate about yesterday, and the elders are on their way as they are claiming Ren stole Lennox's mate," Jace informs us as we fill our plates. I roll my eyes, then give Ren a worried look.

"Dan always told me to stay away from the elders in case they tried to use me or do tests on me." I try to keep eating, but it's turning to ash in my mouth,

"We won't let that happen, sweetie. The elders changed last year. There is now a mix of creatures which will help matters." Lily soothes over her teacup.

Thankfully because Ren and I are still minors and the cops are human, they only ask us to confirm what Dad and Uncle Nic have already told them, as soon as they head out with my DNA and a copy of the police report from my attempted rape including the CCTV of the most recent attack, Alma turns into a taskmaster, even Liam and Nate jump to, to get the house tidy. Lily and I head to the kitchen. We have two days, maybe, so we work on stuff that can be part-cooked and then stored. Ren, Brayden, Kodi and Jace head out for some meat. Bas and Timber set up some rabbit snares, then start tidying outside, hauling dead trees from view.

The next day is much the same, minus the police visit. Matt checked his emails in the morning, then he and a very pissed off Nate hide in one of the offices. They tell us later that Matt's old supervisor had tried getting into his computer and changing the finder's commission from him to her. Matt recommended that Nate put out a check on everyone in case she had done with any of the others.

I slept with Jace that night, but other than kisses, nothing happened. I woke to the feeling of two bodies around me, and then one disappeared with a thud. With a chuckle, I left Jace and Creed bickering and wrestling and headed to breakfast with a smile before going to the old sun room, which is now my studio. I had the urge to create today, flicking my music on as I get set up.

After painting a mountain background, I get sealing wax out, heat it, and use it as a dabber on my canvas. I start making dragon scales, creating a replica of Dan's dragon. The canvas I picked is so big that I have to keep using a step ladder for parts of it. As I set out to paint Elise standing on his curved wing, petting his snout, Liam, who had quietly been watching for the past hour, speaks.

"I always forget how fascinating it is to watch you work, and I am annoyed that I can now see so much of your father in you. I hate that I missed it," he chuckles, but there is a sadness to the tone he uses.

"Do you plan or just create?" he asks, switching to teacher mode. He steps up to the canvas, looking closer at the background. I concentrate on Elise's features before moving to Dan's eyes, not liking the hollow gaps,

"A bit of both", I reply, then side-eye him when I hear the click of a photo being taken. He gives me a cheeky smile.

"This I planned in my head since you taught the technique, something like that." I point to a canvas I did while singing with Trent, it's of a vase of flowers, but look closer and there are hidden images within the blooms.

"I just closed my eyes and went for it with whatever was inspiring me at the time, sometimes it's whatever my music playlist is at the time, sometimes the emotions that are becoming too much. I missed them today, so I wanted to make a memory. Well, kind of." I wipe the tears from the admission to their loss, clearing my throat as I continue.

We are quiet for a while, he's looking through my other stuff, and noises are coming from him. I try not to guess if it's like or not; he was my teacher, so it is sometimes hard not to expect him to grade my work. I inwardly snort, thinking of coming in here one day and finding sticky notes with grades and comments on how to improve.

Half an hour later, Liam has retaken his seated spot, so I decide now is the time to bring something up. I haven't been able to work out how to approach him about it.

"Dan and Elise left me their 'human' effects when they passed away, I have a property I want to use when I turn eighteen, but when I looked, I have a problem, I own the building, or will own it, on my birthday, BUT, the land is owned by someone else, so I need permission to even step onto the drive, let alone do any work on the house." I grab the file and hand it over,

"Want to sign off so I can start bringing my future house up to date?"

He looks over the details with a frown and then chuckles,

"I will agree if you do an art show with some of these, even if you donate the money to charity." I look at him, then look at my feet

"I can't until I turn eighteen and have access to my money to buy an ironclad pseudonym." As if waiting for an opening to enter, Nate walks in,

"I will pay for a vampire one for you. I owe you eighteen years of birthdays and Christmas as your godfather, so I will be happy to." I blink at him and then sigh. I know I'm not going to win this argument.

GROUP CHAT MADE – ART
NATE, MATEO, DEVIN, LIAM, MILES ADDED

13

ME: I need to sort my artwork
out for an art show, you lot are
Now in charge of it. I will mark
the ones I don't want to sell,
And Miles needs to pick what
He wants for the new house.

I put my phone away and let them sort stuff out, and they all soon walk into my studio. I continue with my painting, adding yes, no, and maybe when they hold up my art, a couple of them I just want to burn, but Liam smacks the back of my head with a rag, so I just shrug those off from then on.

CHAPTER FIVE

JACE

"I want to take the next step with Ember, but I don't know how." I say as I close my brother's door, he glances up from his laptop, giving me an odd look that I don't really understand, which is odd between us; we are normally in sync.

"When you're making out or whatever, or even tell her you want more but don't know what she likes – she'll help you, or I can tap in and join", he wiggles his eyebrows at me, but I'm already shaking my head.

"No, I want our first time to be just us. I just don't want her to think less of me, as I have no idea what I'm doing." I hang my head. Creed goes to say something, but the door slams open,

"Jace, your clothes are on your bed, the Elders have been spotted two towns over, and not that I was eavesdropping, but Ember won't make fun of you. Remember, one of her mates is Jenson." Miles states while walking to Creed's closet,

"He's right. Just talk to her, I'm jumping in the shower." Creed pats my shoulder on his way past, and I wince when I realise he was lying in bed naked on his laptop when I walked in. I head to my room to get changed. I contemplate showering; if we all smell fresh as daisies, they will know something is off.

"Miles, I am not wearing that either. Come pick something else, or paint-splattered dungarees are what I'm wearing," Ember yells from her room. Miles flies out of Creed's closet, dumping clothes on the end of his bed and charges with a fierce look that would even have Nikoli quaking in his boots. I eye the clothes he has given Creed to wear, thankfully, Miles hasn't given us matching, but mine do seem on the smarter side than Creed's.

As I go to head down, Miles and Ember are still bickering.

"Miles, I would be more comfortable in slacks. I've seen the guys walking past, and NONE of them is close to matching the cocktail dresses you keep trying with me." Lily brushes past me, where I'm standing at the door, and I lean on the frame, watching as Ember and Miles glare at each other.

I have slacks and a button-up, but I was given Vans to wear. Creed was given cropped jeans and a maple leaf print linen button-up. Lily is wearing a Maxi dress with autumn leaves falling on it and a row of trees around the base. Lily comes out of Ember's closet with a pair of Dungarees with feathers all over, a royal blue tank and a pair of blue DCs.

"Get changed, then I will do your hair while Miles does simple makeup." Lily uses what I've come to know as her teacher's voice. I see Miles' shoulders drop, and he mumbles out.

"I don't want them to look down on her." Lily pats Miles' cheek, making him look at her.

"If she were in a cocktail dress or anything too fancy, they would know she had run upstairs and changed, which could then make them think she was hiding something," she speaks softly as Ember steps into the bathroom to change.

"You've made the rest of us seem casual but befit of our rank, if you put Ember in something she isn't comfortable in, that's going to show, plus, if things turn bad, she can't kick ass in a tight-fitting cocktail dress without flashing her panties," I say softly but with a smile at the end, Miles nods and I get a small chuckle from him as he starts putting away Embers dismissed clothes.

Lily braids one side of Ember's hair, adding more feathers. Kodi and Bas bring in and secure the slide that Kodi made for her, leaving most of Ember's wild curls free, probably knowing Ren will undo it all if too much is controlled, Miles gives her some winged eyeliner, a brush of mascara and some lip balm after passing Ember a Royal Blue pair of prop glasses he heads out to check everyone else, she turns to me and smiles shyly, she doesn't like being centre of attention but keeps finding herself there.

"You look beautiful, Luna", I lean down to whisper in her ear,

"Next time, you stay with me." I pull in a shaky breath,

"I would like us to seal our bond, but I'm nervous and don't know...."

She cuts me off with a peck to my lips,

"We will work it out together," She whispers. Then, she grabs my hand with another peck, and we head downstairs.

"They are at the gate, and it's all of them, plus their guards," Luc states when we are halfway down, then sticks two fingers in his mouth and whistles, which is followed by whoever is still upstairs shutting doors and following us down, Ember grabs a sketchpad out of a draw, which seems to have appeared all over the lodge and sits down and starts to draw the lake, the more she does, the less her handshakes from her nerves. Ren sits on one side of her, and when I notice Brayden twitching, I move so he can sit on the other. He gives me a thankful smile, and she bumps her shoulder into him, her eyes not leaving what she is doing.

CHAPTER SIX

DECLAN

The only ones who seem relaxed are Liam, Nate, Grumps, Lily and somehow my badass baby sister.
I've met some of the Elders a few times, the current ones are better than the last as they are a few hundred years younger, they took over two years ago when we 'dad's unit' proved half were part of the trafficking ring we took down, the vampire elder was caught tongue deep in a child, and he was also dick deep in another's throat, Still, he claimed he was framed, yeah, Lucky for us, we have enchanted body cams that show spells or any charms and what people's auras are, we also had hundreds of witness statements.

I notice Ember take a breath and relax even more when the Elders start to step out onto the deck, wondering what she smelt, I take a deep breath and focus on the Elders, Ember drops the pad onto the table and smiles at a person I don't recognise, She is tall, toned curves, with dark hair pulled into a classy updo, black skinny jeans with electric blue heels and a matching silk blouse cover her body, as Ember steps closer I inhale again 'fuck an Elder is my......' I give Bas a panicked look, and he smirks at me, shaking his head, Timber chuckling at his side, 'Thanks for the support, assholes. '

EMBER

"Victoria, I didn't know you had taken an Elder position," I say, stepping into the Demoness's embrace. I notice Dec freeze and get a look of panic on his face,
"It was a last-minute change. Lock found his mate and knocked her up the first night, he turned into a hovering nancy and couldn't make meetings." She rolls her eyes and then glances at my big brother. Well, I guess we are keeping it in the family.
"Vic, let me introduce you to my Twin brother Brayden and his matcc Miles, Bramley and Mateo." She shakes their hands, with a curious smile on her face.
"My older half-brother Bastille", I tut when I notice Bas is once again making himself appear less huge, and he stands to full height, making Vic laugh,
"My brothers do that too, it's so annoying," she chuckles,
"And this is my oldest half-brother, Declan. I will introduce you to my mates later." She shakes Bas's hand but gives Dec a small smile, then raises her eyebrow at me.
"Guys, this is Victoria, Evans' younger sister." After that, they all give her a warm welcome, and I duck out to let Victoria and Declan gaze/glare at each other.

Ren takes my hand, and we step beside my dad, who smiles warmly at me, before introducing us to whom he's talking to.
"Ember, Alpha, this is the Vampire Elder Wolfgang" He's dressed in linen trousers, a matching top, and grey Converse; he looks like a surfer with blonde shoulder-length hair and Sun-kissed skin. I shake his hand and get a lip twitch in return. Dad then guides us around and starts to introduce or point out the other Elders,
"Becky is the Succubae Elder, and Damon is the Incubi. They are married." Married, not mated, so they are a political match. Becky is stick thin, tall, with no ass and fried eggs for tits wearing a see-through dress, she looks like a younger version of Mrs Sinclair, I give a polite smile and nod, Damon I try not to startle when I get a good look, as he's an older male version

of Lily, I don't get chance to acknowledge him, as he storms off in her direction, thankfully, Liam and Nate are already nearby. I turn back to Becky and notice she's eyeing Jenson.

"Leave my brother alone." Ren growls, his body tensing, ready to jump between them.

"Touch my mate, and I don't care if you're an Elder; there will be a problem," I state. She snorts and heads in the opposite direction. Bram, noticing the same thing I did, rallies his mates, and they Velcro themselves to Trick.

Dad clears his throat, guiding us to the next person,

"Elder Rhett, it's been a few years," Dad says as I look at the newcomer. He's 6ft 5, as broad as Bram, and has similar markings to Darby.

"Mr Shield, it's nice to see you again, and under better circumstances this time." He double-takes at my words.

"Wow, I didn't recognise you, but we must reminisce before I leave."

I smile and nod when he steps over to talk to Darby. Dad raises an eyebrow at me.

"He was at Elise's funeral," I say quietly, and he nods.

Ren squeezes my hand as the next Elder approaches,

"Elder Blair represents the mages, she's an oracle," Dad states, she's the only person who looks old with white and gray streaked hair, with gold, copper and silver threads woven in an intricate design adorned with pearls, her skin is covered in laughter lines, she looks like Helen Mirren, I blink at her but there are subtle differences for her to not be the actress. I bow my head and feel Ren mimic my action; she smiles softly at us.

"Your troubles are ending, my dear. I will leave my address with the lovely Alma so you can put me on the mailing list for signed copies of your books. I would also like one of your paintings. I will let Alma know which one, as you are yet to paint it." She gives me a cheeky wink and heads over to Alma, Dad, and Ren have matching shocked looks on their faces but manage to snap out of it.

"Elder Knox is my name, as your supposed father seems shocked by the old crackpot, I will introduce myself," The nightmare says, holding his hand out, but when I try to shake his hand, he jolts back, and his hand smokes from the burn.

"Humm, brave of you to try and touch another's mate, lucky for you, only one of my nightmares has marked me." I click my tongue, and he glowers and disappears into the shadows.

A small man appears, followed by Trent.

"Hello, I'm Elder Colin. I knew your mother, but I would rather have that conversation in private." I nod and take his business card, and he quickly shifts into a robin and flies away. I don't know if I ever want to know his view on my mother, but maybe one day.

A bouncy guy swaggers up. He's only 5ft 9, but he's as broad as Timber, with a beaming smile, ripped jeans and a Stone Sour t-shirt. Before we can react, he pulls me into a hug.

"Where have you hidden Uncle Reggy, Sparkplug? I was hoping to catch up, you've changed a lot from the photos Auntie Natty sent over." He lets me go with a beaming smile.

"There's a bike event going on, so they are flat out at the garage. Even Pops must pull his weight; it's just down the road." I manage to chuckle.

"Oh, hey Paxton, long time, no see." The guy moseys off towards Pax with his hands in his pockets. I laugh. He's so much like Ryland, it's amazing.

"His name is Daniel, the pup always forgets to introduce himself."

a Polar Bear shifter says, holding her hand out, she's built like an Amazon goddess at 6ft, with dark skin, plugs, and piercings covering her ears and nose,

"I'm Jessica, the Predator Elder. It's nice to meet you, Miss Ivanova."

I try to smile, but it's the first time I've been called that, so my emotions have tripped trying to decide how I feel about it. She nods at my dad and Ren, then heads over to Grumps. The last member steps forward, and I feel Ren go on guard at my body's reaction.

"Madam Celest", I say and tilt my head in faux respect. She was the house mother at one of my group homes. She was never cruel, but she did dismiss me for being human.

"Miss Ashes, you have grown, and I see you embraced sin instead of sacrifice to let your mate find a partner worthy of them." She sniffs at me and heads towards Becky 'Talk about sin,' an Angel and a Succubus being besties is a new one.

CHAPTER SEVEN

MAKAYL

My daughter will have a few problems, mainly the Angel, Nightmare, Incubi, and Succubae Elders, but that is only 4 of the 11, so not terrible odds. Declan is deep in conversation with the Demon Elder and looking panicked, but my mate looks stressed, so I head there. Dec is a big boy and will yell if he needs help, noticing Ember smirking at her big brother. I guess I don't need to worry about him too much.

"It is time for you to come home and stop being selfish. You have already disgraced our family by breaking the contract with Lord Atticus to shack up with a Knight when you could have bedded a future King, now, I find out you're whoring yourself to a worthless shifter, that isn't even the pack Alpha." Damon's words silence the area, and I hear titters from his wife and the Angel, both smirking. I step next to Lily and bend my arm so she can take it.

"Prince Liam and Sir Nathaniel saved my life from starvation; neither wants a mate, and I welcomed the friendship. And until Alpha Makayl, I had not partaken in a physical feed since my rescue, and even that took time to get past my reactions to a male touch, we will be mated soon, and I will not be returning home for you or Father to sell me off to the highest bidder just so it will increase your power, I suggest you leave if that's all you want." I hear Ember mutter something in Latin, and Celeste's eyes go wide and then her top lip curls at my daughter. Within seconds, the scary demon trio, as my children call them, backs my daughter, and my little girl raises her eyebrow at Damon.

"Fine", Damon mutters, then storms out. His wife, realising he will leave her behind, hurries after him, closely followed by the Angel. Lily takes a long breath beside me, her body sagging against me slightly.

"I love you, you're safe here," I whisper to her, something I have to do in the dark of night when no one but us knows there are monsters in the shadows of her dreams. She reaches up, softly kissing me, then turns to Alma.

"I need a Jenson-sized hot chocolate with the works, please," she smiles at Alma, which makes us all chuckle, especially when a few hands shoot up wanting one as well.

DECLAN

"I'm not asking for now." I sigh. I can feel her pulling away, but I am happy with friendship until she is ready.

"Can I have your number so we can be friends first? My baby sister has taught me women don't always need protecting, so I won't get in the way of your job; she would kick my ass if I tried." I release the breath I didn't realise I was holding as she takes my phone,

"Can you give the squidget my number, too, please?" I blink, then realise she means Ember, who slinks up next to Victoria.

"I have to warn you, Vicki. If you deem him worthy, I need to get some payback on Big Brother, so I apologise now." I freeze and look at my sister wide-eyed.

"Payback how?" Victoria asks with an intrigued look on her face, holding my phone back out to me.

"Well, brother dearest smashed into the room while I was sealing a bond with one of my nightmares." I feel my cheeks heat.

"Evan should spar with him to defend your honour, just like my big brother did with my nightmare mate, too." I swallow loudly at her hinting that I should fight a demon warrior; I never want to see the evil grin aimed at me on my sister's face again.

Victoria is cackling and snorting, which is so cute. One last snort is heard as the whole place goes deathly silent and looks at Lily. Ember whispers something, and the scary demon trio backs her. Let's hope she doesn't go offering my ass for a beat down tonight.

EMBER

I summon them as a shock factor, knowing that none of the guests, except Vicki, are aware of our relationship; the three Elders quickly leave.

"Thanks, guys" I turn, not expecting the sight behind me, Ishi is, of course, Suited and booted and looking perfectly pressed, Evan is in ripped jeans and an Aqua t-shirt, stating he's a Barbie Girl he does have a few blood smears here and there, then there's Angel, he's in Boho trousers with doll heads all over with XXs for eyes and an open Hawaiian shirt, and Smurfette toe socks. He also looks like he took a swim in a vat of blood; he's currently licking a machete clean of blood with a Cheshire cat smile on his face.

"Fuck's sake", Vicki scoffs behind them, making them spin to face her, which turns her into a deer in the headlights.

"Dicky, we've missed you." Angel squeals like a three-year-old girl and tries to pull her into a hug, which has her trying to use Declan as a shield.

"Shishter, why ere?" Evan whispers, moving around Dec to her side.

"The Elders were called in about a spat between two packs. We were closer to this one, but will go to the other as well." Vicki states,

"I'm not hugging you when you're covered in worm blood, hello, bro."

She says to the trio, kissing Evan's cheek and hugging Ishi. Angel pouts, which increases when he holds his arms wide to me, and I shake my head.

Daniel, the hellhound Elder, bounds over, asking Angel about the worm while Vicki and I update Ishi and Evan.

Angel and Daniel head home to chop up the Worm meat and freeze it for eating later. Ishi and Evan stay for an hour, and after I drop in that Declan is Vic's mate, and they give the appropriate threats, Dec is an amazing shade of greenish white.

Ren and I head off to join Trick for snuggles, but I do hear Dec mutter to Bas.

"Try to find a mate that isn't besties with our evil baby sister", I chuckle and wink at them both.

CHAPTER EIGHT

JENSON

I slept on and off. My twin and brilliant mate were there to soothe, reassure and, in Quinny's case, hug and kiss me back to sleep.

Lily is looking into their relationship with Mrs Sinclair; she thinks that at least both are aware, as there was too much recognition in their gaze. It's 5 am, and I don't have it in me to try to sleep again. I slip out and head to the shower, washing away the sweat and bad memories.

A small hand runs up my spine, and then a forehead is pressed to my back. I'm not as tall as my brother, but Quinny still doesn't reach my shoulder blades. I feel a press of lips to my back and sigh, turning so I press my back to the tile. Quinny is gorgeous normally, but naked in my shower, all her strength on show. She's breathtaking. She kisses her bite mark over my heart, then kisses down my body.

"Eyes on her *brother* banish the memory of anything but her." I hear my twin say, opening my eyes, I hadn't realised I had closed them, as Quinny settles on her knees, I give her a nod with a shaky breath, and her pink tongue sneaks out to lap at the precum on the tip of my cock, I groan at the feel and cup her cheek, which thankfully she takes as an okay as I don't think I can speak right now, she slowly takes me in her mouth, swallowing when my tip reaches her throat, then pulls me free lapping at my tip and then repeating her actions.

"Quinny", I pant, and she hums around me,

"I don't want to cum down your throat." I manage to gasp out, still pumping my cock in her soft hand.

She husks out her question while looking up at me.

"Where do you want to cum, my Trickster?" she licks her lips,

"My tits?" another lick to my tip,

"My ass?" she squeezes me,

"Inside her dripping cunt?" My brother smirks at me. At his words, I snatch her from the floor and sit on the ottoman, placing her on my lap, straddling my hips.

"Ride me, Quinny." I take her mouth with mine, noting I can taste myself on her lips, she guides me to her core, and as she slowly lowers, my cock twitching with every inch that sinks into her tight warm hole, my eyes roll back releasing a drawn out low moan, I cup her hips with my hands kissing her nipple where I left my mark, moaning out her name as she starts to roll her hips, her perk tits rocking with her movements, I suck her nipple into my mouth, running my tongue over my bite, one of her hands fists my hair the other moves to her clit,

"Open your mouth, baby." Ren moans next to me, she does, and it only takes him a few pumps into her mouth before she's moaning and swallowing him down, kissing her deeply, with a pat to her ass, she starts to move faster on me.

"Take what you need, Quinny, Gush on my cock", and she does with a scream that echoes around my bathroom. I pull her flush with me, stopping her movements as she milks my cock, and our bond clicks fully into place. When I notice she's passed out, I carry her back to bed.

REN

My twin and Luna fall back asleep, but I decide to head to the gym and give them some time alone. Declan is there, pacing, so I throw some hand wraps at him, climbing in the ring, wrapping my own hands as I wait for him. Neither of us exchanges any words as he climbs in.

We exchange blows until we both tire. I glance at the clock as things start to slow, and I notice we have been at it for two hours. "Thanks" he rasps, then heads for the door, I do some basic cool-down stuff before heading to my room for a shower, I can hear Ember and J as I pass, and as tempted as I am to join them, I have to remember she has a lot of mates and I have to share individual time with them, after a quick shower, I dress in dark Jeans and a dark blue Henley that has 3 buttons at the collar, kind of wish it had more so I could leave them open to show off Embers claim on me, I fire off a text to Miles to see if he can find anything.

While Jace and I eat breakfast, we talk about plans for our pack house and decide to call a pack meet to determine what we all want from it. Bray and I need an inside gym, but I would like an outside dirt sparring ring, even if it's in an old barn or something. I know Xander mentioned he wanted a ward like medical area, not that we are expecting pack wars but when the last happened they were treating people on the dining table, he wants to act as a shifter doctor, humans have injections and such for kids as they grow up and we've found similar things for shifters are available but down to the pack doctors to administer but most are old and don't see the point, but having shifters have a rabies and flea shot would help a lot, Bray and I got a bad case of fleas when we were younger that we caught off a wild deer we'd hunted, the human school sent home a letter that we had lice, we had to wait a week for the doc to get the small bottle of medicine to get rid of them, and the shampoo Alma made smelt of rotten leaves.

Jace and I get an essential list, but that's our guess of what people want. Jace needs a library and office, and I'm guessing

Ember and Mateo would enjoy the library, too. What we don't know is if the guys are planning to work from home or have outside business areas they will work from, I guess because Nic was never in a rush to move us out, and we are welcome to stay as long as we want none of this has crossed our minds until Ember, My mate, Our mate came and changed our future dreams, definitely for the better but changed none the less.

My dream before she appeared with Mika was to graduate and then find her at all costs, yes, I want my MMA career, but I wanted her in my life more since the night she was taken away from me, an emptiness lived inside me, it's why I'm constantly reminding myself that, her other mates need time with her, she isn't just mine, but I know I steal more than my fair share, and until one of them calls me on it, I don't care.

CHAPTER NINE

BASTILLE

It looks like I will be the last to find my mate. I'm not sad, but I am worried I will be like Uncle Luc, who is still waiting or in a similar situation to Uncle Nic, whose mate died when they were young.

Tim has told me not to worry. It will happen when it is time, but I can't help mine or my bear's feelings.

I'm currently hiding in Ember's studio, staring at her fantastic work. My baby sister is amazing. I shift my position to look at another painting and startle at my tiny sister.

"Sorry, *baby sister,* I didn't mean to startle you." She smiles at me, ignoring the fact that I was startled, not her.

"It's okay. I was looking for you, actually, I didn't know I would find you hiding here, in any case! Are you okay?" I give her half a smile and a nod. She frowns slightly but doesn't push, putting her laptop in front of me.

"I've spoken to Dan's lawyer and asked if he can arrange early access to one of the properties Dan and Elise left me in their will" She turns the laptop to face me,

"I got these sent this morning. He can give access for work to be done, but I can't move in until I turn eighteen. He said that he didn't mention doing it, but having staff live there so the older ones could move in and be listed as live-in security." I chuckle at the loopholes she's found. It's a beautiful building, and most of it looks like the original work.

"It's an hour's drive from here, but only a twenty, maybe a thirty-minute walk through the woods. Could you and Timber come with me and look to see how much work needs to be done? I know it doesn't have electricity, and I'm unsure about indoor plumbing, even though bathrooms are listed, I was thinking solar panels and a hydro generator on the river to make it as eco as we can?" I nod along with what she's saying while swiping through the photos. She hands me a notepad with a sketch of the aerial shot. There is a main cabin, and some smaller ones with barns; she's covered everything. I chuckle, she has been randomly asking Tim and me things over the last week or so, and peeking at the plans we have on jobs we have been doing, so she has various things marked that we would normally have to add ourselves.

"This building might be the first and easiest sort." as she points to the outbuildings, she lists their uses, a cabin for the litter, a Barn to convert for the scary demon trio, a cabin for Bray and his mates, a cabin for a housekeeper that she wants a greenhouse attaching to, a pack hospital with accommodation above for Xander, a workshop for Kodi and a huge Garage for Pax.

"Maybe ask Liam if he has any trusted staff who want a promotion within his household for the housekeeper position. I recommend a few cleaners too, even if they are part-time like Uncle Nic has here, they live on the outskirts of town but only do two days each, they all have a second job doing something in town." She gives me a nod and jots down a note on another page. I perk up when she says that if trees are fallen or need to be moved, we can use them for whatever, she would like a couple of trails between there, and TripleMoon cleared, as it makes sense.

Timber and I plan to open a sawmill and use our own products when we fully launch our construction company, so her offering is a huge help, but it does mean we need to find one to rent until then, but that's not a problem. We agree to head over tomorrow morning after the guys go to school, Em wants a basic plan in place before she tells the guys, I head through to find Tim but find a moping big bro with mooney eyes and a pout because Victoria left without saying bye, just a note, yup glad I haven't found my mate yet, my bear chuffs out a chuckle at my thought.

EMBER

After Bas leaves, I start to sort which paintings are personal, which are undecided and those that can definitely go. I'm just looking through a pile that I'm not sure whether to just chuck on the bonfire, as I don't know if I like them, when Matt storms in and makes me squeak, as he's not normally one for storming and raising his voice.

"The client's contract states they do all artwork..... that is not for you to decide, just because you think you can do better, which you will fail at, print the art that was supplied I will be passing this hiccup onto Clark and Mr Prince", he hangs up the phone swearing a bunch in Spanish, he eventually flops on one of my chairs, running his hand over his face and hair, closing his eyes he takes some deep breaths when his breathing is calm I speak.

"If you need a distraction, those are unsure, those are sell, and these are burn or not," I say, pointing to each section. I see him send a text, then he snorts at me,

"I know your job isn't my artwork, but I also trust your judgement,"

I say, carrying a few more things over to the sell pile, I got my stuff from storage delivered, so all my high school and college pieces are here. I may do a few extras for the show, but looking at the stack, I don't need to.

"It's okay. You're right, I need a distraction, what are these?" I glance over at his words.

"They're sketches or pieces that would need frames", he hums, fires off another text, then starts to split the two piles. Miles, Kodi, and Nate walk in shortly after, the former two looking at the canvases dotted around,

"What's happened now? I briefly read your text before Clark rang and ranted," Matt tells Nate to meet him at his office, then turns to Kodi and Miles,

"These all need to be framed for Ember's upcoming art show because of the rustic-ness of some of her art. Reclaimed wood frames would look amazing, same as displaying some of the canvases on wooden ladders rather than easels. Can I leave that with you guys while she finishes sorting? Miles, you also need to decide if you want any for the house" Matt kisses my crown and drops a peck on Miles' lips, as he heads off. Kodi picks up a thin canvas.

"Do some of these need frames? This would look good with a driftwood surround." I glance at the canvas, it's a painting I did of a beach I lived near, I left off the beer bottles and discarded needles and added a northern lights-type sky and some mermaid tales.

"Yeah, sure, there are some Post-it notes on that table if you guys want to mark what's happening to stuff," Kodi asks if he can steal a scrap of paper, then grabs some Post-its and makes notes on sizes and types of wood.

"Is Mateo okay?" Miles looks worried,

"Yeah, the artist at the publishers decided his art was better than mine and ignored that my contract states I do my own artwork," I shrug, and we share an eye roll before he starts looking through what needs framing.

Alma brings lunch through and shortly after Kodi and Miles head of to the local salvage yard, the place is apparently an Aladdin's cave as they collect unwanted furniture or if someone dies with no will they empty the house, some items are tarted up and resold others are there so people can do the tarting themselves, I give Kodi a list of things I want for the new house and neither question it, I decide to curl up in one of the old arm chairs and start doing the preliminary sketches for Lily's new club, she's opening a pleasure bar, humans will see it as a BDSM club members only, but it's mainly aimed at incubi and succubae as a safe space to feed, she is having a heaven and hell theme, but wants some same sex couples and groups not just male-female which other artist tried to push on her, she also wants a huge one done of the main Doms, Dames and Subs. I will have to meet them to get a fair likeness; a photo doesn't show mannerisms. I'm actually wondering if it would be easier to do it on the wall at the club rather than on a canvas.

I feel I'm not alone and look up to see Rhett staring at the Canvas I did of Dan and Elise,

"You can touch but use the backs of your fingers, not the pads, as you will melt the wax," I say, not moving but acknowledging he's here. I can see him startle, not expecting me to notice him, it's then I notice River hovering in the hall, obviously not trusting him to be alone with me,

"I'm guessing the talk you wanted with me wasn't a reminiscence," I nudge, wanting this conversation over.

"What do you plan to do with your inheritance and the items Dan left you?" I see Uncle Nic and Liam walk in, both annoyed and on guard,

"Not that it's any of your business, the items I was left were Dan and Elise's PERSONAL items minus a few books that have been put in the family vault, the same with the money and properties, none are from the family name, just theirs so what I do or don't do with the items, money and properties is of no matter to you," I stare at him holding his eye, I'm not scared of him, he is of the family but from Dan's record he only has 122 gold scales,

"BUT I plan to live off the interest of the money, donate some of the larger buildings to charity organisations, most are already rented out to one thing or another anyway, with the charities Dan and Elise set up themselves, two of the largest buildings are schools that work with orphans and have scholarship funds to get into higher education,"

I still can't work out what he's after, but thankfully, Uncle Nic steps in.

"Any of her financial questions should go through her father or me if he is deployed before she turns eighteen, or Ignatious Salvatore as the estate lawyer," I see a flash of fear go through Rhett's eyes,

"Is this being sold at your art show, I heard mentioned?" I shake my head.

"Pity" Then he strides from the room, followed by a guarded and scowling Uncle Nic,

"He will be the last to leave! May I?" Liam glances around, and I chuckle.

"Like I could stop you" his smile is akin to a child in a candy shop; he goes around oohing and arrrring and muttering, then adding Post-it notes. He stops at my Wax Dragon,

"Would you be willing to do something similar but less personal?"

I smile at him as he takes a step back.

"Maybe smaller, humans don't have as large walls to fill nowadays, which is a shame, large pieces always felt more satisfying," he gets a far-off look for a short time before looking at me,

"I've ordered some more wax. I plan to do three smaller ones for the show once it arrives," he says, pleased with the answer.

He then plops down in the chair beside me, grabbing a sketch pad and watercolour pencils, and we both work in silence until we are called for dinner.

"It's been ages since I have just done it for fun rather than to teach or commission" he doesn't seem sad, but he does seem more relaxed than he has been.

"Liam, not that I don't enjoy your company, but do you plan to open your own house here, or are you moving in permanently?" Uncle Nic asks as we enter the dining room, and Liam turns in mock upset, 'Ah, there is my dramatic art teacher',

"Before Liam starts down a Shakespearean drama scene, we are closing up and opening here, but we are waiting on their schedule as we moved it forward ten years", Nate answers, shaking his head at Liam.

CHAPTER TEN

EMBER

The next few days pass similarly, minus the guys being at school, Matt agreed to help with my art show and as I will be doing under a pseudonym for my art he takes it as a branch and claims it as two clients, him and Nate had a little tiff when Nate tries to pay him for two clients, I manage to calm things and have him get a finder's fee then he gets a percentage of my sales that goes into a college fund for his future kids, as Liam and Nate's companies are linked it's easier to explain away, as Liam supplies artists to Nate on occasion.

There was a paperwork issue, so we would be technically trespassing if we went to the cabin until that's sorted. On the fourth day, I wandered through and nearly collided with Dad and Lily, the latter in full rant mode with her arms waving in all directions and keeping out of arms reach of my dad.

"You know the kids don't like it when mum and dad fight", I state, and get a 'what the hell' look from both of them,

"When you've hate fucked it out, can I have a word, mother dearest? Please?" I hear some expletives leave Dad's lips as I enter the kitchen, and Lily giggles before replying,

"Just because you speak it in Russian doesn't mean you can talk about your father like that, sweetheart" I need to hold in my laugh at Alma, the oldies and Trent all eavesdropping. I raise an eyebrow, and they attempt to scatter.

Trent looks like I'm about to cane him.

"Day off?" I say with a smile.

"No waiting on the General, we have some stuff to check out that could be linked to the lab," he sits and eats the sandwich Alma places in front of him, while I sip my tea, I fill him in on what I remember of people and the companies I remember them using until a freshly showered dad walks in who grabs a to-go cup of coffee kisses my crown and heads off with Trent who is stuffing the last of his lunch in his mouth as he follows.

When the guys get home, their usual routine hits, and they all sit to do homework, well, minus Jace, who heads up to his room. I grab him some of the snacks and take them up to him, but he just mumbles a thanks and shuts the door.

The next day, I finally got the okay from the lawyers, so once the guys left for school. Bas, Timber and I head to the new property. I checked with Ren the other day if he minded that the property could be solely in my name, but he preferred it. If anyone managed to challenge and win against him for Alpha, all they would get was the pack name, and that made sense. The house is mine, not the packs.

We decide to walk through the woods, where there is an old, overgrown dirt trail, agreeing to open it enough to get a small vehicle through, like a 4-wheeler.

When Timber shifts and Bas throws what looks like a saddle bag over him, then tells me to climb on his own back, he shifts, lying down for me. I giggle; it doesn't take long at all to get through, and where some trees have fallen to cover the trail, they easily climb over the top. As the trees seem to be more spaced, the guys shift back so we all step as humans into the clearing. I quickly snap a photo on my phone, and the untouched beauty is just amazing.

The lake is smaller than TripleMoon's, the deck has rotted and collapsed but all the floor is covered in wild flowers like a meadow, the main cabin is also smaller and a lot older, it has what looks likes carved portions to the wood, there are five cabins and four barns between us and the main house, then three cabins and a barn on the other side of the lake. As we make our way to the main house, I take photos of some of the flowers and send them to Alma, then recommend that she come up and see if any need saving before Bas and Timber trample them.

Bas or Timber dip into each of the structures we pass and only one is beyond saving but the foundation we might be able to use, Timber leaves to check the building on the other side and Bas goes to check out the access road, when they get back they walk around the building checking everything out, most of the windows even though we will replace with better can be salvaged for something and only one is cracked where a branch has fallen against it.

"The cabins on the other side have been updated more than these, and looks like the Barn has already had some done to make it into a house, so your plan should work," Tim tells us and Bas confirms the drive needs a huge clearing before we can look at the state of the road, we work through the house leaving Post-it notes on most of the doors, it has four floors including the basement which is only three rooms but takes up just over the full plot so we can easily split it up, I don't even class it as a basement really as one side that's facing the lake has a door level with the ground, I point it out, and ask if we can turn it into windows it would be a great gym.
We head back and get washed up before the guys get home from school. I'm hoping Jace is happier, or at least ready to tell me what's upset him.

CHAPTER ELEVEN

KODIAK

When we wake up Saturday morning, a text is waiting in the pack group chat.

ANGEL: Guys, you need to be in
hiking scruffs today, Trent, Marcus,
James, Calum, Xander, Saint, and
Paxton, that means you guys, too.
I've okayed it with your bosses.
Miles and Kodi, bring some notebooks,
If you're not down by 930, then you miss
out and don't get a vote.

MILES: When you say scruffs?

ANGEL: I mean, we are going for a
walk to where it will be dirty and dusty
don't wear pretty clothes. *Eye roll emoji *

Most of the guys have given thumbs-up emojis or confused GIFs. I jump up, throwing on my work boots and Jeans, I stick on a nicer t-shirt than what I wear when I help Tim and Bas, but I still stick a flannel on. I don't need a winter jacket even in the snow, but I do, as humans notice, we maintain a little of that in the woods, in case humans spot us when we are hiking.

Ember, Bas and Timber are packing up coolers and flasks when I get downstairs, and the guys are all sitting grumping and chugging coffee, even J has coffee mixed with his hot chocolate.

Mateo has an amused, if not tired, look, and I wouldn't be shocked if he knew what was going on.

I raise my eyebrows when I notice Bas loading up tools in some hiking bags 'Why not drive?' I finish my breakfast quickly, and I'm just finishing my coffee as Ember steps in,

"Ready, guys? Some of you will need to help carry stuff, please," she smiles at us all,

"Sweetheart, I've got a few ideas, let me talk to them and then get back to you, the top of the list may need some help getting out from parent control, but I think she needs it", Liam says as we pass, and Ember gives him a thumbs up.

"Luna, what are you planning? As Alpha, I should be aware, but even my Betas look confused." Ren asks, and Ember just gives him a smile and heads outside, a heavy bag on her back.

With Bas and Timber walking on either side of Ember, leading the convoy, I chuckle when Miles starts to grumble,

"It's thirty minutes, if that, Miles, shift if you want, but trust me, please" A look passes across Miles' face at her words, but he doesn't grumble again.

A few guys that aren't carrying anything shift but stay behind Ember, I notice Bas and Tim marking trees and catch up to see if I can help,

"I think three trails would be good; this one is pretty direct and then two more scenic ones," Tim's gruff voice reaches my ears, and I notice Ember agree.

"Will you be able to use all the trees? I don't like the idea of waste"

I love that she gives a shit about this stuff, and Bas tells her about a sawmill they have a contract with, they give us a discount, especially if we book a two-day session with a lot of material, and they plan to set up their own to have as the supply for their construction company, but it's finding the land.

"Is it land you need or capital?" Ember isn't looking at either of them, and she looks nervous.

"Land, we would need to be near a sturdy road and preferably near trees we can use. We plan to replant so it replenishes. Nic has said we can use trees from his land, but we still need space," I reply.

"I would like to do custom furniture and carvings and have a shop linked to the mill so we could do with somewhere that is seen rather than hidden." She nods and walks for a bit before glancing at my brother,

"What about near our access road? It's a busy road, and the lot opposite is empty with what looks like an old car dealership, we could convert that into the office and Kodis showroom, clear some trees partway up our road and stick the mill there if you maintain the trees on our land then I won't charge you rent." she shrugs when the guys gasps of 'are you sure?' sounding more like bear cubs than what they normally sound like,

"Yeah, if we clear our road and then clear out your space, get your mill built with those and fix the road, then you can be 'milling' the trees as you cut them to make room for what we need," everything she says has an air of nonchalance to it, we do or don't she doesn't mind but the offer is there,

"If you want me to supply the upfronts, I can, as it would be an investment towards my future. Ignatious can okay it," she says all this as if it's all that easy.

"It's the same as he's signed off on the bill for hiring you guys, the mill is probably a smaller amount" I'm not the only one listening and trips at her words.

"Okay, thank you, *baby sister*" Bas pulls her into his side, hugging her, kissing her crown and whispering brotherly affection, while Tim thumps a palm to my back, beaming about the progress.

A new scent hits my nose, wildflowers, and my Angel starts to bounce. She takes a few steps past the tree line, and then we fan out next to her.

"Welcome to what will become the BloodMoon pack lands" Her arms spread wide, she passes Jace a notebook,

"Sorry, I noticed it the other day, so I grabbed it before we left" he just chuckles at her and takes it, shaking his head. She does something with her phone, then Trent's phone goes barmy. His eyes go wide as he looks at it,

"Alma wants some of the plants saved before they get trampled in the bag you have. There are pots for you to rescue them for her" Trent nods at her words, and we start to follow her to the main house, making sure we don't crush too many flowers, so we don't incur Alma's wrath. The bag she is carrying gets thrown towards Brayden, and Ren lifts her into his arms, her legs wrapping around his waist, as he whispers praise to her and promises rewards for being such a good Luna. I'm not the only one who has to give my cock a squeeze and pep talk.

EMBER

After Ren finally puts me down, Kodi takes my hand as we trudge towards the main house, then Ren, Jace and Bray start planning,

"Through those trees are three cabins and a barn, the barn I plan to renovate for the scary demon trio and their mate, and one of the cabins I plan to offer to the litter and their mate." I start to point and explain my plans, Ren smiles at me, and I hope he knows he does have a voice, even if I am taking the lead right now.

"The biggest cabin here, I thought, would be good for you and your mates, Miles. It's got eight bedrooms. I'm presuming, with the grandeur, it was for visiting Alphas, or the retired one, but it's big enough for your growing family." He double-takes at me, and Brayden stumbles, looking at Ren, who gives him a wink,

"Xander, there are a few choices for you, either three or four bedrooms – there is a six-bed, but I want that for the housekeeper. Trent, Marcus, Calum and James, I was going to put you guys in the five-bed over there, and then when we are settled, or you find your mates, we can build you individual ones" I notice a few awestruck, mouth-open looks at me, but I carry on, pointing things out as I go,

"There are four barns over here, I thought, a workshop for Kodi, another for a med hospital kind of thing" I'm counting them on my fingers, but I get cut off by Xander, before I can finish.

"You would allow me to set up a shifter practice here?" Xander is breathless, like he's in shock. I nod, with a frown, but when I get a smile and a kiss on the cheek, I continue.

"Pax I presume you want a garage or whatever so that was another barn taken, and we can do whatever with the fourth, I noticed a dirt-sparing ring in Jace's notebook so we could have that in there, with some more rough workout stuff like ropes and bags, or we use as a dorm house for any extra staff we need, I don't know" I shrug,

Bas and Timber have headed off to mark the trees on the access road, which was what they told me would be their first job.

"We checked all the structures when we came the other day, but be careful in case we missed something, you will need torches as there is no electricity, there are Post-its on doors for my ideas on what should be done and who's room it should be etc, but feel free to tweak anything, it was an initial idea," they all nod but nobody really moves, other than to look around from our spot,

"The huge balcony up there is already marked to be reinforced so you can land there in Dragon form, Darby, and we are going to have a landing area marked out on the ground level, too." I start to get nervous, I've gone wrong, and then Miles starts talking faster than even I can keep up. The guys laugh and tell him to make notes, and then we can sort, or he might get confused if he gives one idea to one of us and a newer one to someone else.

"You okay, Angel?" Kodi whispers in my hair,

"Just hoping this all works out and everyone is happy and all the bad is over." I smile up at him, and he gives me the softest kiss, even when it turns a little heated. His lips are like a soft caress against mine, a throat clearing makes us pull away in a daze, blinking at the others like we have just come out of a trance.

"As hot as this is, I need more information if I'm going to make this place fabulous," Miles' hands snap to his hips, and he taps his foot impatiently with an eyebrow raised. Kodi and I chuckle, the latter heading after the guys to explore.

I set up the camping tables and coolers while Miles fires off design questions at me. We settled on light natural wood and ironwork to keep the feel of the place. Obviously, the gym will have a modern feel, and the offices will be individual to each person.

Even though all will be connected, Bas recommended each cabin have their own power store and then just use the main houses if they need backup. As Bas and Timber come back, they talk about having the same energy setup for the mill, solar and hydro with some large batteries as backup.

We are just finishing up lunch when Nate, Liam and the litter rock up,

I explain to Ryland, Ajax and Cin about my plan and that they can move in once they graduate and after a lot of hugs and a few tears *cough Ryland cough* they head off with a pad to make a list of their requests, theirs won't be a first job, as they still have a year and a bit before they graduate being the school year below us like Bram.

Liam stretches out on the grass next to me, sipping out of a can of raspberry Fanta,

"I have a girl in mind to be your housekeeper, but there is a past there; her mother is the caretaker of one of my properties, the one I was at when I was your teacher, in fact. Esmeralda came into my service just after we found Lily, the house she was born to and served was attacked by mages. Back then, we fought between species a lot. Long story short, she was drugged and raped. We gave those we saved a choice: work for us or fend for themselves. They signed a blood oath to be loyal and never do harm to others when they joined our household." I nod, having heard some of this before, for the contract to be broken, Liam and Nate need to bleed on the contract, then burn it over a blessed flame.

"We found out she and a few others were pregnant, she had Amelia, and we gave her the option to raise her, or we would find a nice home, which most chose the second. Amelia has vampire speed, strength and our long lives, but she has earth mage powers, which is a constant reminder of what happened to her mother. I had some work done on the gardens five years ago, and Amelia met her mate, the son of another of my staff, Flynn, a wolf shifter and Ellie May a crystal mage they have twenty children, Various combinations of their parent's abilities including a few hybrids and most are twins, triplets and quads plus a few individuals." my eyes widen, but he chuckles and continues,

"Their eldest, Jacob, well, he prefers Jake, is Amelia's mate. He's a wolf shifter/earth mage hybrid and can use his earth abilities in

his wolf form." Ren comes over and pulls me into his lap,
"Let me guess, mummy dearest forbids the relationship as he's not a vampire." My voice is cold and sharp, which makes Nate chuckle as Ren kisses my temple, feeling my annoyance.

"How'd you guess?" I smile at Nate and sink more into Ren's touch.

"Hugo, Gus, Robin and Seb were the year above me, at school, they are Jakey's youngest siblings, they were always talking about a lemon-sucking vampire denying their brother his mate and how sweet Ammy was, but they never mentioned how many siblings they actually had." I chuckle at the memories of the pranks they told me about. When I see the fondness in Liam and Nate's eyes, I expand,

"Dan found them playing hide and pounce in our yard and made them promise to look after me at school. Ellie was friends with Elise; they had a knit-and-natter group, which was more drinking spiked tea and eating cake, setting the world to right." Liam and Nate seem to relax at the link to Dan and Elise. I glance at Ren, and again, he kisses my temple, but he seems to understand my feelings,

"We would like to meet them both or even video call, are we going to have much fight with the mother?" he voices my main worry.

"No, it will be more her trying to guilt Amelia back once she finds out, if you do a blood contract with Amelia, then her mother won't be able to, Amelia doesn't have a proper contract with me as it's linked to her mother's, so it is an added piece of paper in a way, but I can authorise the transfer and countersign her contract with you two," Liam states and Nate gives me a thumbs up.

I can see Ren in thought, but I get an idea,
"Get Amelia and her mother to come here and look around, then her mother can feel like she's part of this if we word it that Amelia is helping me set up house and home for my Alpha and helping me understand my place as Luna, blah, blah, blah from

what I know of Esmeralda she will see it's as a boost in the social ranking of her daughter helping your god-daughter set up home with a powerful Alpha, at the moment the housekeeper's rooms are still there, even though we plan to convert them into a workroom and extra storage for her and her have a cabin, but then her mother will just see what she needs to and then hopefully we can hold off on her visiting. Amelia can send photos, but if she angles it right, her mother won't know the bedroom is in a cabin. If we make hers and the guy's cabins the first priority, then they can move in as security, and she's around to help with cleaning and here when we get deliveries, et cetera," I finish, and Liam is already messaging Samson, his Butler.

"If we get Jake over before the work is done, too, he can help with the landscaping, as I know it's not the bears' strong point. Liam could word it that he's lending us some help, keeping it true by more than Jake coming over, Nic won't mind housing them for now." Ren adds in, Bray nodding in agreement, and it all makes sense to me. We look at Liam, who just gives us a thumbs up, fingers flying over the screen of his phone, the tip of his tongue appearing between his lips, making me smile. He may be one of the oldest vampires still living, but he still feels closer to our age sometimes, like that fun uncle who helps you cause mischief.

CHAPTER TWELVE

JACE

Saturday night, Ember slept in my room, but we both passed out as our heads hit the pillow. We ended the day with a plan in place and were all in agreement on the family rooms of the house, and agreed to sort our rooms and offices ourselves.

Sunday is more relaxed, mostly its filled with talk about getting the area for the mill cleared and that set up and working out a time frame for everything, I manage to ask Ember to stay with me again tonight, when we head up, I get winks and nudges from the guys I know they are just trying to ease my nerves, but I don't think its fully working.

I pull Em into the shower when we get upstairs. As I'm washing my hair, I feel her lips on my chest; she can only reach up to my jaw, so I lower my mouth to hers. When she sucks my tongue into her mouth, I let out an embarrassing moan. She kisses back down my body, sinking to her knees, smirking at how I am looking at her. She pumps my cock a few times before taking my swollen tip into her mouth. Her tongue piercing teases the underside and my slit, my hips move even with my trying not to, it only takes five bobs of her head before I choke out her name as I cum and she licks me clean, then raises herself back to her feet, rinsing the conditioner from her hair, I dry myself and try and recenter my being as I watch her braid her hair, I turn and decide to shave needing another minute, to get my head straight.

She is lying on my bed, and it reminds me of a scene I had read. I decide it might help my nerves to use my books as a guide. She's reading Theirs for the Night by Katee Robert, her fingers slipping into her slick pussy and then circling her clit, I can see her hips twitching as I crawl up the bed,

"Keep circling that flushed bud, and read out loud while I taste you", I rasp out. All the composure I'd had in the bathroom was gone. I slip my tongue inside her, while she continues to read, but it's a stunted read with gasps and moans as I thrust my tongue in and out of her.

She eventually throws the book to the floor, pinching her nipple and clit and crying out as her slick floods my mouth. I lap up every drop.

Letting out a muffled yelp as she clamps her thighs around my head and rolls us, so she is straddling my face. I shift my canines and sink my teeth into the inside of her thigh; another cry leaves her, more for me to lick clean. After I've sealed the wound, she shimmies down my body. Thankfully, kissing me on her way down, I'm lost in her, but gasp and arch as she slides me inside her pulsing cunt

"Fuck, so tight and warm." She rolls her hips and sinks her teeth into my chest, six pumps of my cock inside my amazing mate, and I cum so hard and blackout.

EMBER

Jace goes limp beneath me, in more ways than one, and he starts to snore; he's blacked out from his orgasm. How does he fall into a deep enough sleep to snore that quickly?

His flaccid cock slips from my body, so I move off him, then I quickly clean up in the bathroom and grab a damp cloth to wipe away the bodily fluids that are on him, then cover him up. No one enjoys waking to the feeling of crusted cum all over themselves in the morning, and it'd have to be worse for guys if it's all matted into their pubes and under their balls. The guys are good and tend to clean me up before they pass out. I turn the lights off and slip into bed with him. He pulls me into his arms,

"I love you worm," he mumbles, he started calling me his bookworm last week so I'm guessing that's what he means, I'm glad I had that small Orgasm when he made me read to him, and the tiny one when he bit me or I would be unbearably needy 'shut up Ember you've been spoilt so far' I eventually fall asleep to his soft snores.

JACE

I slowly wake, feeling amazing. I notice the lights are off, and Ember's steady breathing is next to me.

Wait!

Oh fuck!

Shit, I fell asleep!

Asshole!

I slide out of bed and slip some boxers on, padding to my brother's room, I enter, then not so nicely shake him awake,

"Creed, wake up!" flipping on his light,

"Jace? What's up? Is Em okay?" he's rubbing his eyes from the shock of the light turning on.

"Probably not, I'm an asshole, I passed out and didn't even get her off" I flop next to him,

"Go get in bed with her, do your thing, make sure she gets fulfilled like a none-asshole mate should," I say with a whine and glance at him.

"What the hell, Jace? Go hug our girl and wake her with your tongue, if she wakes up and you're not there, she's going to think you regret it" he lies down, pulling the cover over his head,

"Seriously, you're not going to help me?" I ask, glaring at the Creed-shaped lump, as the sheets start to speak.

"Bro, none of us knew what we were doing the first time with her; the only ideas I got were from watching porn. I just listened to Smudge's reactions as I tried what I watched, learning with her, we all have different tastes." his voice is muffled, but I can hear the snap of his voice. I sit for a few minutes and can hear him sigh,

"Come with me, please. I will talk to her, but be there to help me, please. I licked her, but I don't think I did enough. I got distracted by the way she felt and forgot please," he rolls over, glaring at me. I must look pitiful enough to him,

"Please", I whine again, and he finally nods, and we head back to my room, climbing in on either side of our mate.

CHAPTER THIRTEEN

CREED

I wake to the sound of soft talking, I can't believe my idiot brother came and tried to hide in my room instead of talking to Smudge, I get it, he's embarrassed that he didn't get our mate off and he passed out from the orgasm she gave him, but seriously he can't be the only virgin to do a fumbled three pumps and pass out,

"Jace, I don't expect all my mates to be pro porn stars with the stamina of rabbits, as long as you talk to me and don't hide, just think we can have lots of practice." Goddess, our mate is perfect,

"I've been feeling inadequate with how the others have been in bed as it is, so it's nice to know it's not just me, erm, why is Creed here again? I thought you locked the door!" I'm lying on my back, but smirk.

"I was hungry and hoped I could have a pre-breakfast snack," I kiss her shoulder, running my hand down my chest, taking the cover with me, then stroking my cock,

"Let my twin lick that gorgeous pussy" My eyes are still closed, and I give my cock a squeeze.

"Then when he has you dripping, I'm going to fill you up while you swallow him down your throat," I feel Ember's lips press against mine, once she's on her knees and elbows,

"Slip your index finger inside, brother, while you suck her clit," Her back arches, and I hear a sucking noise.

"Lap her clit like it's a dripping ice cream and add a second finger," My voice has a purr to it, and Ember's eyes roll to the back of her head.

"That feel-good smudge?" she can only nod,

"Shift your tongue and fuck her with it while running circles with your wet fingers on her clit." Ember's mouth opens,

"That's it, Smudge, let my twin tongue fuck that greedy pussy of yours." She's forcing herself not to ride his face,

"Yes, Jace, mmmmm, fuck yes," she bites her lip,

"Pinch her clit, bro." I know when he does, she lets out a gasp and a low moan, and his hands both fly to her ass as he laps up her release.

I tap his shoulder, and we quickly switch positions,

"This is going to be fast, smudge," I thrust inside her, making her gasp out my name,

"Watching you ride my brother's tongue, fuck you have me right on the edge, fuck our mate's greedy mouth brother," I start to fuck into her with long, sharp thrusts, forcing myself deep with each one. Ember already had her tongue sticking out for Jace.

EMBER

"Fuck your mouth is almost heaven, only your pussy beats it," Jace gasps as he and Creed thrust into me with a matching pace, Creed's tail joining in by fucking my ass, I scream around Jace as Creed slaps my clit setting off my orgasm, I can feel him filling me with hot spurts of cum, soon followed by Jace filling my mouth, I swallow it all down and then flop to the bed, I feel a warm cloth and then hear them talking.

"Thanks for guiding me, brother,"

"Sleep, Smudge, we've got to go to school."

"I love you, Worm. Sweet dreams," I finally blacked out.

CHAPTER FOURTEEN

JACOB

"Ma, the master has asked me to go help on a property his goddaughter is fixing up. Do you know where my hiking bag is?" I yell while digging in the junk closet under the stairs, which used to be a toy closet, but Ma added a sunroom where she has the grandkids' toys now.

"It's in the quad's room. I'll pack you up some food. Where are you staying?" I give her a vague idea, as he didn't give me those details, I step into the doorway of my youngest brother's room, and only Gus and Seb are around.

"Is my hiking bag in here? I have a job I need to pack for!" Seb, being the unofficial leader of their group, jumps up and dips into the closet, then hands me my bag as Robin stumbles into the room,

"We need to pack, guys! We're coming with you, Jakey. To help Emmy out," Mom appears in the doorway looking confused,

"Elise's Ember? You said the master's goddaughter," I shrug, I have no idea what's happening, I never do with my youngest brothers, Hugo steps around Mom, kissing her cheek, his phone pressed to his ear,

"Yeah, Emmy, I got it. Are you sure it's okay? Yeah, that makes sense! Yeah, good plan! See you soon, bye," Hugo hangs up the phone and looks at Ma.

"Ember has a family, but her social worker hid it when he found out. She has a grandad, a dad, two uncles, two older half-brothers and a twin, plus she has ten mates. Miss Volks from school is her dad's Mate, and one of her uncles is the Alpha for the TripleMoon pack, which is where we will be staying.

Apparently, the Master is kicking himself for not linking her to her father." Ma has tears running down her face. I don't remember the girl, but the quad talked a lot about her.

"The property is one Dan and Elise left her in their will, one of her Mates is an Alpha and she needs help setting up the place ready for when they turn eighteen, but none of them knows anything about landscaping other than chopping trees so she's 'borrowing' some of the master's staff to help," he does the action for quotation marks around the word borrowing, I frown. "Word is the master has recommended Amelia for the housekeeper position to get her away from the battleaxe." he steps into the closet, grabbing his own stuff, all four of them packing bags. I'm just staring, mouth hanging open,

"Amelia is visiting with her mother next week to meet with Ember about the job, the idea is for it to be a brief visit as there is work happening on the house still, and then the master is sending L.S.V (lemon-sucking vamp) to check over the maintenance of his properties overseas while Amelia gets settled and have a contract with Emmy, not the master" Hugo says, Ma is watching me closely.

"Emmy said she and her Alpha mate will support your mating if it's what you both want, and you have a permanent job there if you want it, but that's on the down-low till L.S.V is out of earshot." Hugo goes on to explain that Ember called, telling them to come too, as it can be explained away that us five aren't really needed on the estate, so the master could spare us, as L.S.V always looks down on us, she will believe the words of a future Luna.

Ma wipes her face, then heads off for extra supplies for the five of us. Now, it's not just me. I can't believe this girl is using favours from Prince Liam to help Amelia, and I can finally be together. Hugo turns and raises an eyebrow at me 'What? Oh yeah!' I head off to my room to pack.

I'm nearly done when Pa steps in, placing some boxes on my bed, "Pack the things you don't want Ma and me looking too closely at and seal them up, and we will pack the rest and bring it over once you have your room sorted" I do as he says and I'm kind of thankful if Ma found the letters Amelia and I have been able to swap over the years she wouldn't try to stop herself reading them.

"I have messaged the Master, I will send a group of five down to help that are a mix of skills, from what he said the place hasn't been touched since Dan, Liam and Nate, killed the corrupt Alpha in the 1800s" I give Pa another nod before adding one of our old books to my bag, maybe there are some rare plants on the land. As I head downstairs, I spot one of my brothers.

"Let's take two jeeps just in case and hitch one up with a trailer with some basic tools and one of the ride-on mowers, anything else we can get while we are there." They all agree. Yes, they are still immature at nineteen years old, but when they want to do something, they give it their all, and they are loyal to a fault.

I end up with the trailer and all the bags, while those four just drive themselves, I guess it gives me a nice four-hour drive to think over what is about to happen in my life.

The main thing that is running through my mind is that Amelia and I will finally be together, no question in my mind that it's what we both want. The only problem we have ever had is the control her mother has over her life.

CHAPTER FIFTEEN

EMBER

As per usual, the Quad rolled in like a swarm of mayhem, Seb proceeded to dibs a cabin over by the litters, while Jake, Hugo and Gus helped clear the trees for the access road.

I should probably call it a drive, as that's what it is now, or will be. Seb and Robin started on Amelia's and their cabin, ripping out anything not needed, so it was basically an empty shell. They picked the six-bedroom cabin so when their parents visit, they can stay there and also until Amelia is ready to seal the bond. Jake is going to stay with them, so there isn't any extra pressure on her.

We have been getting stuff delivered to TripleMoon, and then River and Saint have been bringing stuff here with their shadows, so the solar panels for the quads, Amelia's, Xander's and the other guys' cabins, are all here and going to be installed soon.

Miles already has paint and some furniture on order. He's currently talking to Jake about their cabin, the kitchen and bathrooms needing updating, like who has a brown bathtub, really?

Bas and Tim have a friend who owns an electrical and plumbing company that sends out a few guys. I don't know if they've worked with Jaylen before, but he is the one currently on site, and he sets me on edge. Saint is sorting security in all the buildings, Dec, and he plans to set up a security firm when they get bored of being in the force.

Timber and a small crew are erecting the Sawmill structure today and the hydro generator is being built in a few days, all of the fallen trees from the drive and the ones around the main house were taken to their friend and they had enough there to build the full mill and some storage areas, all the machines are coming the day after tomorrow, so once the roof is on, the solar panels fitted and the hydro generator is up and running, they will be ready to go.

Things are moving quite quickly now. The Quad sat Bas and Timber down three days after they arrived and asked if they could set up a sister company, and when they do big jobs, they will do a discount on the landscaping side. Kodi has been flitting here, there and everywhere, and they all agreed to finish our place before they build the showroom and offices.

I'm just finishing the last touches to what will be Amelia's bedroom, Jake's mom snuck in after they left and sent me photos of how she had decorated her own room, Miles did a quick shopping trip for paint as we were just going to leave cream walls and let her do it herself but cream is boring, her walls ceiling and floor were cream but she had sky blue bedding and a rug and a vase full of wildflowers so we went with it.

I try not to react as Jaylen steps in as my phone rings.

"Hello", I keep him in view but don't stop what I'm doing as I answer the call,

"We are heading over now, walking, so we will be there in twenty minutes", I confirm with Nate. I heard him before disconnecting the call.

"What's up, Jaylen?" I ask with a smile. I don't feel nervous, but I also don't like how he's blocking me in the room.

"Oh... Erm... electrics are done, I'm heading to the other cabin."

I nod, not understanding why he's telling me this. Tim and Bas are in charge of the site, so it's them who need to be told. Hearing movement downstairs, I relax a little more.

"I wondered if you want to get a drink with me later?" he goes for a smirk, I think, but it's more of a grimace, thankfully, Hugo appears,

"I would think her brothers and mates would have something

to say about that dude," I see anger flare in Jaylen's eyes, as he storms off.

ME: Do you have another electrician? Jaylen just asked me out and was pissed when Hugo pointed out I had mates x

BAS: Fuck's sake, yeah, I'll give Taylor a call, Jaylen works for him, so I will request a switch and explain why x

BAS: You good? x

I apologise to my big bro, which he shoots down, reminding me it's not my fault, and something about fucking dick-less pricks needing to leave his sister alone. I turn to Hugo with a small smile.

"They are on their way. Can you let the others know and keep an eye on Jaylen until his replacement arrives?" Hugo agrees, tapping away on his phone, and we head over to where people are starting to get their lunch from the coolers. Jaylen's on his phone, his face goes from annoyed, to okay, to pure joy.

"Yeah, that's great. Is he on the way now? Brilliant," Jaylen grabs two subs and four bottles of water, then walks off. We hear him talk to one of the other guys on his team, but he ignores Tim and Bas,

"I'm off, I've got another job, someone is coming to replace me, I think," Bas stares at his back, open-mouthed, as we munch on our food.

"I've got most of the land plotted. There are a few wild animal dens I'm guessing you want us to avoid and leave them be?" Seb asks, breaking the shocked silence, and I nod, finishing my drink,

"Yeah, when the new guy gets here, get him to check cabin seven and then check Jaylen's work elsewhere, we need to start clearing the outside space for the greenhouses" Robin points to himself and Gus and I nod, not minding who does what, just that it gets done.

"I've dug up some more plants to save," Hugo mumbles around his apple, and points to a collection of pots. Jake gives a distracted humm,

"I've got more greenery to clear around the barns," Jake adds, watching the treeline,

"Did we decide where we are putting the compost pile?" I ask.

"No, but we could use that collapsed cabin; the base of the cabin has sunk, and the floor is rotted, but will give a foundation for a wall around the base," I nod again, and a couple of Bas' guys offer to help

"Once the paint is dry and the electrics checked, this cabin is done, just needs filling with furniture," I add, head tilting towards cabin seven.

"I'm going to start ripping out the kitchen and the bathrooms in the main house; it's mainly painting and electrics in all the cabins now."

Bas lets us know. I wondered why he was covered in dust.

"Any idea how many greenhouses we need? Or what type? Veg and fruit? Herbs? Potion stuff?" I glance at Jake, but he's packing up his stuff, and I notice Trent breaking through the trees with Liam, Nate and two females.

The severe-looking one is dressed in a floor-length black dress with long sleeves and a high collar, and her hair is in a tight bun. The younger is in a knee-length version with black tights and court shoes, her hair is still in a bun, but a looser one, uniform, something I know Liam doesn't insist on. Amelia has a guarded look on her face. Jake storms off towards the cabins as Trent breaks away and bounds over. We agreed to keep Jake away and make Esmeralda believe he's given up. I have a letter to slip to Amelia if I can from him.

Trent halts in front of me, hugging me.

"What can I do? Did you know you have paint everywhere? Again!"

He laughs,

"Yeah, I was getting cabin seven finished, find Miles and find out what furniture we have on-site for it and get it inside, please. Then we can sign it off and move the focus to another." He nods and bounds off.

Liam and Nate both give me hugs when they reach us, the quad gives the females dirty looks and then heads off to do their jobs. Again, this is all on purpose. I'm just hoping Amelia understands.

As Nate introduces the women, Esmeralda tries to control the situation by not letting Amelia have a voice. Timber's Grandfather, Trunk, is helping to restore some of the items inside and manages to distract her for me.

"We would appreciate your view on the housekeeper's quarters, Alma, the TripleMoon housekeeper offered, but it's a much larger pack, and she hasn't yet found the time, but as you are here…" She follows him through the kitchen, and Bas and I share a smile.

Amelia relaxes a little, but I need her to relax more.

CHAPTER SIXTEEN

AMELIA

Mother isn't happy that Miss Ember is only seventeen and is in scruffy clothes when she is meant to be the Pack's Luna and the master's goddaughter.

"Thank you, Trunk", Miss Ember mumbles, then directs me outside and away from Mother. She takes a deep breath when we are away from the main building.

"I'm going to be honest, we are not a traditional pack and probably never will be, the Alpha, one of my mates, is aiming for an MMA career, one of his Betas, my twin, is his trainer, the other Beta plans to be an author, in short, most of the pack has careers already or have plans for them, some plan to do college when high school is over, some are already working, being a few years older than us." She looks at me to see if I'm following what she's saying, and I give her a nod.

"I'm an artist and author. I will need someone to remind me to eat when I'm lost in a creative project, as a house, we need someone to cook most meals and oversee the household. Alma, my uncle's housekeeper, has trained the boys into a pretty good routine, and we all agreed we would stick to it and adapt slightly to your way. I'm not saying your training is wrong, but it would probably be easier for you to train a slightly different way than to train ten plus guys to do it another way.
Alma has offered to let you shadow her for a week or so, and she will always be just through the trees if you need her help." Again, I give her a nod as it all makes sense.

"To start it will just be us, Me and my ten mates in the main house, that cabin will have my twin and his three mates, that cabin will have four single guys, there are three cabins on the other side of the lake, one will not be in use till next year and the other will house the quad as they are setting up a sister business with my older brother." She gauges my reactions, but she won't find much, as I know how to conceal things from my mother; we carry on walking.

"Jake asked me to give you this." She hands me an envelope, and I quickly tuck it into my pocket, forcing myself not to snatch it from her, smoothing the fabric again.

"Eventually we will get extra help for cleaning the house and cabins, and I will ask you to sort the rota for the extras, but for now we plan to do our own laundry and general cleaning, on top of meals we would ask you to do a deep clean of the bedrooms and bathrooms once a month, even if you spilt the rooms over the month and keeping the main rooms downstairs tidy, your spare time is that, and yours for what you wish. If you want to curl up in our library and read, you can," I stare at her in shock, but she isn't focused on me right now.

"This cabin is to be yours, well, yours and Jake's if YOU choose to seal the bond, the contract you sign with us will take you from Liam's employ and your Mother's rule." We are standing in front of a cabin,

"Jake has decided to stay with the Quad until you are ready, but he is to be taken on as our groundskeeper," I notice Jacob not too far away, near what looks like a collapsed cabin. I crave to run into his arms.

Over the last five years, we have had a few stolen kisses and soft touches; there has to be a catch to all this.

"As you won't be entertaining like a normal pack, what else do you expect of me?" she plops down on the porch step, and I follow her down, tucking my feet under my bottom, making sure the skirt of my dress covers everything.

"As long as the housework and cooking are done and you throw food at me throughout the day, for all we care, you can pose for nude photos, just nothing illegal. Alma sews and sells her quilts in her spare time, she also donates cakes to local fairs but that time is up to you, I've said the same to Jake and will when we take extra cleaners on but with them, the cleaning will be in exchange for a roof over their head whereas you and Jake will be paid as well as a roof over your heads. I'm not saying we will never entertain like a normal pack, as those things will probably happen at some point," she gives a shrug, and we both watch the guys near Jacob for a little bit.

Realising I can speak freely with her, I decided to test the waters a little,
"Is topless a rule, or am I allowed to wear t-shirts?" I hear a thud, and then Jacob is staring at me red-faced, Ember bursts out laughing, and I join her in the merriment.
"I would prefer no nudity outside your own cabin in case we do have visitors, and it also may cause problems if your mate keeps killing people for looking at your tits and ass," Ember chuckles out, and I hum in agreement.
"You also won't be expected to wear the uniform, this is smart for me, I'm normally in scruffs, covered more in paint than not when I'm in my studio, the guys are similar, again something more formal if we have visitors, but you do you."
We chat a little longer, I want to look around what will be my cabin, but it makes things too real, and I'm scared. She tells me about the rest of the people in the pack, for a time and about being at school with the Quad.

"Miss, Jake needs your opinion on a few things" Miss Ember hops up, and we follow the guy over. She mumbles,
"This looks more than a compost heap", which of course, with Shifter hearing the guys, all hear,
"Yeah, we worked out we could save some of the cabin and turn it into a groundskeeper storage house, it also means I can clean up in there if I get to muddy and don't traipse dirt and stuff through the cabin", Jacob says, but he doesn't look at me, I try to look around, but I get lost in thought watching him.

"Ammy", he whispers, then I realise most are watching me,
"Sorry was thinking about the job offer", I feel my cheeks heat.
"You're to be the housekeeper. What greenhouses do you want?
Just basic veg or more?" I glance at Miss Ember, but she's also
waiting for my answer. I duck my head and mentally calculate,
"Erm… oh… I guess if there are twenty-plus people daily, we will
need a large one for veg. Would it be cheeky to have one for fruit
and one for herbs? And maybe a flower one," I look in Ember's
direction, but at her feet, not her face.
"No, it isn't. Would you just want to plant fruit or trees, too? We
have a blood dragon and a vampire; both have fruit smoothies
with blood in them multiple times a day. When they have kids,
they will need some too," Miss Ember informs me. We never
talked about species, which surprised me; she only talked about
the person.

"Go big, better to have free space now and be able to add more as
more people and kids arrive," she tells Jacob,
"The housekeeper's rooms are being turned into storage so we
can make a drying room for flowers and herbs for you." Again,
this young girl surprises me by wanting to offer so much and
thinking of the future not just right now, I hear Jacob's deep
chuckle and I fight off the shudder, knowing my body is lighting
up for him, Miss Ember makes a note of supplies on her phone
but as she's putting it away her stance changes to a more formal
one.

"We have allocated cabin seven for you to stay in while the work
gets done here, I'd like you on-site to be there when rooms need
cleaning the landscape guys are staying in a cabin over the other
side of the Lake so they won't bother you, you won't be cleaning
their cabin until they leave, and a couple of our pack are moving
into that cabin for security so you won't be alone." She states
enough truth, and I realise Mother is making her way over with
the master.
"What do you mean while work is done?" My mother snaps, and
the change to Miss Ember makes me double-take.

"The main house has no electricity and the water only goes to the kitchen sink, this guest cabin just needs furniture and a few last-minute checks, I want Amelia on site so that as rooms are finished in the main house they can be cleaned and furniture moved in, she is also on-site to take in any deliveries, plus if the site team has questions about the kitchen, laundry or any other aspect of her duties she is the best to answer them, what would I know about cooking? My Alpha would like to start moving in when we turn eighteen, so we want this renovation to go quickly and smoothly." I can feel her dominance leak out, and I notice Mother flinch; the guys with Jacob have also gone ramrod straight.

A dragon swoops in and lands on the other side of the lake and then shifts. It's not until they get closer that I notice the dragon has a rider. Another guy appears with a pop-up table, then grabs a box and a tool belt and walks into my cabin. I twitch, wanting to follow him, but I turn, focusing on Miss Ember.

CHAPTER SEVENTEEN

EMBER

Ignatious and his assistant Jimmy walk over, they shake hands with Liam and Nate, plus Jake, as he's the highest ranking there. Ignatious nods at Amelia and then pulls me into a hug. Jimmy looks shocked but shakes my hand.

He goes over the contract I asked him to work out, highlighting the benefits and role Amelia is to perform.

"Jacob, my boy, can you sign as a witness, please?" Jake quickly washes his hands in the water bucket, drying them on a cloth he pulls from his pocket, and signs on all the parts Jimmy points to, "Ms Rose, would you countersign, please?" Esmeralda looks smug, but it turns to annoyance when Jimmy points and flips the pages too quickly for her to read. Jimmy slips the new contract into a locked case, and Ignatious pulls another from inside.

"Jacob, I need you to sign this to confirm that you are happy for Liam to loan you out until the work here is done." Trent and Amelia countersigned Jake's contract to work for us; we had already gone over it with him.

"Are your younger brothers around? So, they can do the same. When Jake points to where they are, he says he will do them before he leaves. Jake sends them a text, so we don't hold them up; it also needs to be done when LSV isn't around, so Liam and Nate can blood their contracts.

"Finally Liam I need you and Nate to blood this contract to release Amelia Rose from your employ," he pulls an old oil burner from his bag and places it on the table, both Nate and Liam slice their palms and hold over the old contract, the words written in blood and a thumbprint of Amelia's at the bottom, the date shows she would have been five years old.

"It has been an honour to watch you grow into the amazing woman you are today, little Ammy," Liam says, I watch as Esmeralda gives Jacob a smug pleased look as if she is getting her way, as Ignatious holds the contract over the blessed flame Bas walks over, the contract spits and hisses and a blue flame turns it to ash.

"How long until the drive is done?" I ask my brother.

"Two weeks until it can be used, three until it's done, why?" I hear Esmeralda scoff. I turn to Amelia,

"Can you be packed in two weeks and then spend a week with Alma learning the guy's likes and dislikes, ready to move in when the road is safe?" She nods, ignoring her mother.

"I don't have a car, though, so how will I get my stuff here?"

"My brother could," pointing at Bas, I start to say, but am interrupted by the Quad arriving.

"Pa is coming over in a few weeks to drop off another mower; you can come with him." Amelia nods at Gus as I hear Esmeralda grind out

"Can't be her brother," but we all continue to ignore her. I'm not sure if it's the bear or his Cherokee heritage she has a problem with, but I don't care; she won't be a problem once she is off packlands.

"If Mrs Greenbriar can help that would be most appreciated as I don't want to take Mother away from her important jobs, and being able to load my books into Mr Greenbriar's truck would probably be for the best", Ignatious moves away to get the quad to sign their contracts, Bas and Trent countersigning them – they all already hold my signature, like with the house being in my name Ren decided the staff would be safer that way too. Trent passes me a tote bag, and I thank him.

"This is all for you", I pass it over to Amelia. Her mother is starting to look bored and annoyed again, but again, I don't care about her.

"They are on our family plan, and our resident tech genius has created and installed an app that you can meal plan and do shopping on all in one, the phone has all our pack numbers as well as Ignatious and some of TripleMoon pack as they are family when you turn it on you will have to add security information so only you can use it, anyone else tries they will be arrested as there is pack information on it. If you get stuck with anything, call Darby as the tech is his baby." I notice her mother looking at the tablet.

"If you want to use it as a normal tablet, you can; the only thing monitored is our apps, you won't be able to screenshot or copy anything on those, but you can use your own email and other apps. I think Candy Crush is already installed." I chuckle and watch her mother again, and she has a calculating look on her face.

"We only supply the phone so we can contact you. We will be notified if you turn them off when we try to call or if you ignore a call. Darby can check if you have a signal, so please answer if we call." Her mother now looks annoyed again, but Amelia looks delighted.

I say goodbye to Amelia and pull her into a hug, but her mother just stomps away, not even a polite farewell 'How rude!'

"Remember ALL our numbers are on there, don't hesitate to reach out," her eyes dart to Jake, and I give her a nod, and then she hurries after her mother.

CHAPTER EIGHTEEN

DEVIN

Since Ember started on our home, it's been a whirlwind of stuff happening with setting up the Sawmill, getting stuff cleared and picking décor, even though the latter we left for Miles, just giving him 'hell no' occasionally.

Mika gets back from his deployment tonight, his and Lily's mating ceremony is tomorrow, Ember and Amelia have spent so much time trying to keep Lily calm, then Elder Victoria turned up, and they all got drunk and watched sappy movies and things seemed to even out again the next day they spent going over details of the ceremony which also distracted Miles for a bit as he was getting stressed about things not turning up and delays.

I've had Ember in my bed the last few nights, but tonight is the first time we've been alone, normally Darby or one of the guys dips in, I feel ridiculous how possessive I am over her blood, today I ended up having an odd conversation with Victoria about it, she wanted to know what to expect from Declan, she differs from humans as she has only one, two week period a year, it's also the only time she can get pregnant.

The thought of my delicious mate pregnant has me hard in seconds. We're seventeen, so I shouldn't be thinking that, and I don't think I'm ready to be a dad yet. Some packs are still run by the old ways. At sixteen years old, you get your marks, find your mate and start a family, and a cabin on pack lands is allocated to you.

I will admit the number of packs run that way is small now due to humans frowning on teenage pregnancies, but Ember has finished school and college, her career is starting, and two of her mates are four years older than us; we have also not talked about how it will work. Will we all be dads, or will the others be uncles? Some of us are ready and happy for babies tomorrow *cough Ren, Saint cough*, and some are shit scared of the idea, still, we all have the injection Xander gives us to avoid accidents. Ember's scent hits my nose, and I move down, slipping my tongue between her folds, lapping at her syrupy goodness,

"Devin" she sleepy moans, knowing she's now awake I sink my fangs in either side of her clit, arching her body off the bed as her orgasm hits, I use my vampire speed and I'm balls deep inside of her before the peek truly hits, I then make slow love to her, other than shared pants and moans there is no other noise in the room, I cup her ass and tilt her hips giving me a deeper angle making her gasp and her cunt clench around me, her hand finds my ass pulling me deeper and harder into her body, her hips rocking with mine, one hand moves to my hair fisting it and pulling my mouth to hers forcing me to swallow her cries of pleasure, her nails have broken the skin on my ass, and I can feel a trickle of blood, I bite her lip making her bleed in our mouths,

"Cum for me! Milk my cock!" the minx bites my lip, causing our blood to mix, and I lap at her mouth, the taste setting off a string of orgasms for both of us.

"I love you," she whispers as we come back down,

"I don't think love covers what I feel for you," I reply, my cock still hard inside of her. I carry her to the shower and continue to show her how I feel.

EMBER

When Devin and I head downstairs, I find Amelia curled in a chair in the hall, tears trickling down her face, Devin kisses my temple and dashes off, I roll my eyes, guys can't deal with girls in tears, I sit next to her, the chairs used to bracket the old wired phone but now it's just two chairs and a table with some pretty flowers, she slides her phone towards me.

> MOTHER: You are not getting any younger,
> You finally have a high-level job,
> even if it is with an unknown young pack.
> I have sent you information on a few
> respectable mates that could help
> That pack, pick one, or I will.

I reread the message twice, shocked at the words, then looked down the list of names. Declan is one of the names, but has a question mark next to it; all are vampires, though. Victoria walks over, and I pass her the phone. She goes down the list, mumbling.

"Pompous dick, gay, gay, should be dead, snort, I think he still suckles on his mother's tits, Playboy." The comments go on, then she passes Amelia her phone back.

"Pick Declan, and then we can ditch him and run off together," Lia and I laugh at her.

"You are not under her control anymore, and part of your contract with us is you can't be part of an arranged mating nor push your children into one," She nods, pulling out a handkerchief.

"Ignore her, we will help you deal with any assholes that turn up, so Jake doesn't have to kill them" I fire off a text to Jake's mom to rally the troops as I'm going to do Lia and Jake's ceremony next week, they have both said they are ready but they don't know how to take the next step, Ellie May then sets up a group chat with me, Alma, Lily, Vicki and the quad, making a comment she's not adding her mate as he can't keep secrets and the planning for that begins.

Dad and Lily's mating ceremony is a small affair, well, kind of. Our family isn't small by any stretch of the imagination. We're having a pack meet tomorrow, which is part of the celebration, but tonight is just us and a nice meal.

The ceremony is similar to that of a handfasting, everyone is standing in two sections to create an aisle, and there is a flower arch where Dad is standing waiting, Grumps is doing the blessing, even though it should be the pack Alpha, but Uncle Nic didn't argue. Lily is wearing a simple linen dress that hugs her curves, no sparkle, no shine, no shoes. Lia wove flowers into her hair. She has minimal makeup on and the only jewellery she is wearing is a locket that holds some of Dad's hair, it's an infinity symbol in platinum set in obsidian.

Dad's wearing similar 'not a dress' he has light grey linen trousers and a cream top, again no shoes, his only extra is a chain I made with links of resin that contains Mine, Dec's, Bas' and Bray's hair and an infinity pendant that has Lily's hair inside, Alma blessed both pieces so they won't break and if lost they will return to a box kept in their room. After the meet tomorrow, Vicki is taking them to one of her properties so they can fuck like rabbits without the kiddos overhearing, Vicki's words, not mine. Once the words are said, blood vows and rings are exchanged, we head inside for a traditional Russian meal. Lily commented that she missed some of the foods, so Dad said That's what we will have.

Vicki and Dec are definitely closer. She's spoken to Devin and me about the period situation as hers is coming up next month, but the relationship is too new, and she's not ready for kids yet. Once she leaves, I sit Declan down and explain the situation to him, which she owes me BIG time for.

CHAPTER NINETEEN

DECLAN

I'm so happy for Dad and Lily; she still refuses to let us call her mom, claiming she is not old enough. I love the simplicity of their ceremony; the few I've been to in the past have been ridiculously extravagant and long, similar to those human movie weddings. Thankfully, no drama happened.

I see my baby sister talking to my loony mate, there is no other way to describe her, she randomly pops up wherever I am and asks me random shit, this morning I was sitting on the toilet, and she pops in sits on the sink unit to discuss my favourite flavour of Monster, that thirty-minute discussion ended with us agreeing that Mango Loco was the best, she pecked my lips and disappeared again and I finally, after clenching for twenty-seven minutes, finished my business.

The other night, she shook me awake to ask if strawberry laces were better than flying saucers, see, a complete loon, but fuck, she's gorgeous. We have both agreed to take this slowly. The girls start to walk over, and I hold out an arm, which Vic slips beneath and kisses my lips.

"I need to go; there has been a breach at the gate, and I need to find out who." She kisses me again.

"ACDC or Dolly Parton?" She asks before popping away. I lick my lips, savouring her taste before I remember Ember and glance at her

"Can we talk in private, please?" she nervously asks. I nod, putting an arm over her shoulders, and we head to the TV room. She's twitchy and won't look at me.

"You're making me nervous, baby sister", I try to chuckle, but it falls flat,

"Vicki asked me to talk to you about her period," Em says, and I now get why she's nervous. I avoid eye contact and nod.

"Demons have a single two-week period each year; it's the only time they can conceive. Well, they can conceive for four weeks, a week before, and a week after. She's coming to spend the night tomorrow, but after that, her ovulation starts in three days, she's not ready for kids, and you both are taking it slow, she said, for that month next year, it will be a joint decision." She takes a few breaths.

"Xander has said he is happy to do tests to see if your contraception would work against her, but again, not a risk for this year. Evan takes her someplace below and guards her while she sees to her own needs" We sit for a few minutes.

"Is it the same time every year? My birthday is in five weeks, and I want to spend that with my mate." If we need to be apart every time we don't want kids, it's going to kill me.

"For now, yes, demon pregnancies vary in length depending on a few things. Minimum will be four months, the longest will be eighteen months, her periods will follow the year pattern, a month after the baby is born, but that first one is just a bleed, she won't be fertile"

That makes sense. I give her a numb nod, still stuck on some of the details.

"Vicki's birthday is two days into her ovulation" I stare at my sister,

"Why didn't she say anything?" Ember hands me a list.

"Demons celebrate differently; being born is not an achievement on their part, so it's not rewarded. These are her favourite treats. I messaged Evan for you." I take the list, but I don't look at it,

"What do you mean?" she rolls her eyes.

"She will basically be going through what omegas call a heat, so her battery-powered boyfriend is going to be getting a workout." She ponders something, then continues.

"This is the direct email to Sarah Buzzfree. She changed her name for fun. She makes custom Vibrators and sex toys. She will take a mould of your penis, tongue, fingers, whatever and make a silicone vibrating replica." I stare at my sister, who has an innocent look on her face,

"How? Why? Erm?" I have no idea what I'm asking.

"Email her and say you need a rush and get Saint or River to take you to her; she owes me a favour and has your name on her priority list."

She smiles, a blush covering her cheeks. I just nod and pull out my phone, and the reply hits in seconds. Ember pats my shoulder and leaves.

Saint drops me off with a chuckle, and I sit in a chair in the waiting room, thumbing through the brochure. This catalogue is huge.

They can mould my hands to sit around her ass or tits and squeeze them, finger nipple clamps that twist and squeeze, they can even do my tongue and teeth with my fangs pulsing as a clit stimulator. My order is huge, and I hope one day she shows me how she uses my gifts. Two hours I sit and wait, until Sarah comes out with a black velvet suitcase on wheels.

"All done she's a lucky girl, I slipped a card as we offer the same for the ladies so they can treat their men, we can do all her holes"

She gives me a wink and walks off, I decide I'm going to write her a letter to go with this gift and make a note on my phone to do one every year, god I'm a sap. Saint grabs me after I write my letter, I text Evan, and then Saint sends the two cases to Evan. Ember, my amazing sister, got all the treats sorted and packed in another case.

The pack meet is a little tense, some females did not think Dad would go through with it and hoped they could be the hole he fills to drown his sorrows.

At 21:30, Victoria turns up, we grab some food and head up to my room. After eating she shyly asks if she can grab a shower I put a clean towel and one of my t-shirts on the sink unit, then strip down to my boxers and climb into bed, I play idle bank on my phone while I wait, it doesn't take long before she's sliding into bed and up to my side, we share a soft kiss and whispered goodnights before we fall asleep.

When I wake, I watch her sleep for a short while before deciding I've been sappy enough. I slip out and head downstairs, loading a tray with goodies, then grab a coffee for me and a latte with six sugars for her. As I step into the room, I hear a sniffing noise.

"Coffee and cherry muffins, my hero." She yawns as she sits up, and I set the tray on her lap. I slide behind her so she's leaning against my chest.

"I know I won't see you on the day, but happy birthday, Loony." I kiss her neck as she moans around the warm muffin. We then share breakfast, her feeding me bites of hers, me doing the same. She ducks in the bathroom to get dressed and then plonks on my lap, before she can say anything my bedroom door slams open, Saint's shadows visibly flash across my ceiling and then there is wrapped candy dropping from the shadows including Dracula and devil confetti, Ember fills the door and fires off a couple of streamer cannons and there are yells and cheers of happy birthdays and welcome to the families, then the door slams shut again, then Shadows appear on Vic's lap, and a pink fluffy gift bag appears, she's giggling the whole time, and I'm hoping the confetti isn't in my underwear draw.

VICTORIA

These people are crazy. I open the bag, still giggling, and I can feel Declan chuckling behind me, then grumbling when he realises, he has confetti and candy in his coffee. I start opening the gifts.

- A signed copy of Ember's book
- A leather and feather necklace
- Some homemade fudge cookies
- Ten pairs of fluffy socks, all with devil-related pictures

Declan spends the next hour picking up all the candy and putting it in a bag for me, scooping up some confetti to put in my bags so I have some.

This next month is going to be hard without him, but he's sweet and gives me a deep kiss before I leave, another happy birthday, and I'll miss you.

I arrive at Ishi's house, and I tell them all what Ember did this morning, which has them laughing. We agree that now that we have family topside, we need to start celebrating some of their holidays. Evan decides to do research while guarding me for the next month. I reach my room, and there is a black velvet case at the end of my bed and a purple one on the floor. The black one has a letter on top.

My beautiful Demoness,
I had these custom-made, so not only do you have some relief, but it is a relief I can give you. But please race back to me as I am already missing you being in my arms. Soon, you can have the real thing.

I don't finish the letter, throwing the case open, my core flooding at the sight that greets me, I quickly check the other case, seeing that it is full of snacks I then move the case off my bed, set my phone on a stand pointing at the bed I strip but slip the tank I stole from Dec's closet on, I then grab a toy and push record on my camera, I won't be the only one suffering through this,

"Oh, Declan", I moan as I slip the long Vibrator straight into my core.

CHAPTER TWENTY

EMBER

We set up the Ceremony, and I tasked Miles to get Lia ready. Ellie-May is sorting Jake out, and they arrive as planned. Jake was throwing 'what the hell' looks at his mum, but when Lia appeared at the end of our makeshift aisle, and he saw her, they both froze, a half-smile took over his lips, and he held out a hand to her. It was as if their souls connected before our eyes.

I expected Ren to want to do the blessing as pack Alpha, but he told me it was my idea and my job, so, infusing the blessing with my Alpha Command, I blessed their bond and mating. We decided on buffet food and simple drinks. I start to notice Jake getting twitchy and a blush creeping up Lia's cheeks, so I walk over, handing them the key to their cabin.

"We left some surprises for you both. The fridge and cupboards are stocked. Jace and I took the liberty of unpacking your books, some of which we would like to borrow. There will also be no work done over the next week, so you have the pack lands to yourselves." I don't wait to see how embarrassed I make them; Jake scoops up Lia and heads off to the start of their forever.

We are still to hear a peep from Dad and Lily, and I don't blame them. We know Dad has read the texts and updates we have sent, but none have needed replies, and knowing I'm still floating from room to room with my own mates, I understand their want for privacy.

My sex life seems to have slowed but I'm unsure if it's that they are over the novelty of it or that the knowledge of us not having to rush has finally set in I shouldn't complain, a good dicking three plus times a week and its never just the once with each guy that night so I really have nothing to complain about, and thankfully I'm not walking bow-legged.

Uncle Nic is still fielding mating requests, but they are fewer and farther between. Ren is eighteen at the end of next month, so it will no longer be Nic's job. Our place is getting there, but we have hit a few snags like waste disposal, Bas and Timber have been going slow, so they don't miss anything major, and I've agreed, in a way, that each weekend we go out as a pack and do what we can to help, whether it be painting or building furniture.

I'm currently sitting in my studio sorting out Dec's birthday gift. He has loads of photos in his bedroom of him, Bas, and Brayden growing up; some include the other guys, but most are of them. He commented the other day when Miles was taking a selfie with me that he wanted some with me included, so while he was at the office one day, I snuck in and took photos of the ones he had. Now I'm sketching the original, but including myself in some way, I plan to replace his photos with my sketches and cover them all in tissue paper.
Alma and Creed took some photos at Dad and Lily's mating, so I've got Creed printing them up for me. I'm also doing some others, like a sketch of my graduation with us, Dad, Uncle Nic, Uncle Luc, Grumps and Grandma.
I don't have a photo from my graduation as I just got the certificate in the post, and I've done both high schools, so I included Dan and Elise and also my college one.
I've also done a clearer copy of my book cover for him on canvas, instead of him and me in silhouette, you can see our details.
I've had a few messages from Vicki asking what is considered a normal present for a mate's birthday. When I told her he collects unusual weapons, she was so excited, even her texts were gibberish.

That night, none of the guys asked for me to be in their bed, so I decided to shower and then read in my bed before I went to sleep, but as I stepped out of the shower, I was pulled into the shadows

and into River's bedroom,
"Time to make you fully mine, Firefly."

RIVER

My shadows are already caressing her body. I just pepper kisses over her neck and shoulders, I start to sing The Calling's, Wherever You Will Go to her, making her shiver, and I know that my shadows are driving her mad,

"River, please." As I sing the last few notes, I pull her on top of me.

"Mark me, Firefly." I kiss her sweet mouth, and she follows by kissing along my jaw, down my neck, making my skin tingle with each press of her lips, eventually she stops her lips hovering over my heart and glances at me through her eyelashes, smirking slightly before sinking her teeth into my chest, my back arches, precum dripping from my cock and even my shadows feel like they are pulsing, I don't feel the change, but when my Firefly takes my mouth again her hands grasp my horns, she runs her body up mine, and I can feel her wet core running over my leathery skin and its now my turn to beg,

"Please, Firefly, I need to be inside you." Thank fuck she understands Latin. One of her hands runs down my chest, swirling over my abs, as she pushes to her knees before taking my cock in her hand, stroking the leaking tip between her wet folds.

She pushes down a little, just the tip pulsing inside her as she pumps my cock while licking her lips. Moving slightly so my tip enters and exits her body with her small movements, done with her teasing, I grasp her ass and pull her down, so she is flush with me, my cock filling her fully.

"River, I need to move. I need...." Her words cut off as I sit up, taking her mouth, I start to lift and drop her on my length slowly, using her to pump my cock with her fluttering core, my shadows bat her hands away from plucking her own nipples, and her hands thankfully return to my horns. Somehow, my cock gets harder at the sound of her moans and whimpers, my shadows secure her hair up off her neck, and they trickle coolness across her flushed skin,

"River, please." Her body arches, head tipping back, giving me access to her pulse point behind her ear. I cover it with my mouth, sucking, scraping my teeth over her flesh as she bounces on my cock, sweat dripping between her full breasts, my shadows start to seep into her where my mouth is,

"Yes, fuck yes, River, more." Each word is a gasp, her tits bouncing and swaying with her movements, my shadows are pushing in her ass and tapping against her clit, how do humans please their women without the help of shadows? Suddenly, my shadows fill the room, pulsing in time with the beat of our hearts. I roar out my release, filling her deeply as she screams out my name. I shift back still inside her, and manage to catch her as she passes out.

My firefly is sprawled over my chest, my cock still twitching inside her. I feel my brother's shadows join mine in the room and watch as some move the hair from her face and caress her cheek. "Soppy bastard," I mumble and get a flick to the ear, then his shadows form a hand and give me the finger before disappearing, which has me trying not to laugh, which would end up waking my mate. I fall asleep easier than I have in years.

CHAPTER TWENTY ONE

EMBER

I woke feeling River pulsing inside me, I pepper kisses on his chest, as I push up, supporting myself with my hands on his abs, slowly rolling my hips,

"Firefly?" One of his hands moves to my hip, so I grind on him harder, his other hand cupping my breast before fisting my hair and pulling me in for a sloppy, desperate kiss,

"How do the others not fuck you 24/7 when you feel this good?" I know it's not a question aimed at me, so I don't offer an answer. I'm so close, so I change to swivelling my hips in a circle, which is when he fully wakes and rolls us, so I'm on my back and start to mimic my earlier action of slowly rolling his hips. He kisses over his mark, making my breath stutter and my pulse jump. His hips start to stutter against mine. He takes my mouth, swallowing my moans as my orgasm hits, and he follows me within seconds. We fall back asleep, giving each other soft kisses.

I'm woken by Trick, stomping into the room,

"Your phone has been ringing non-stop for over an hour", he pecks my lips and hands me my phone. I stupidly don't check the caller ID before I answer.

"Tell me your address, I heard you sucked the right cock and are now rolling in it." I blink and glare down at my phone, but I don't recognise the number. Ren walks in with a steaming mug of tea and a small smirk,

"Oi Bitch answer me, you useless, ugly cunt." I see the guy's freeze, and River sits up. Ren places my mug down on the side table and sits beside me, his nose nearly touching mine.

"Baby?" his voice is barely concealing his growl. I sigh and hand him my phone, which earns me a kiss. I hear a scoff through the phone.

"Get the cock out of your mouth, you fucking ugly whore, and give me your address NOW!" I see Ren take a deep breath,

"May I have the name of the guy talking to my girl like he has the right to?" I hear a scoff and a chuckle,

"That dumb bitch owes me for carrying her through the class we shared and were partnered in, the names Swift." I'm frowning at Ren and shrug, I don't know a Swift, wait, maybe I do,

"Razor Swiftly?" I hear a grumble,

"Snake shifter, college science class." I finish my tea, kiss River and then climb over Ren, getting a squeezed ass and a licked nipple on the way. I hear a chuckle from the door and turn to see Paxton leaning on the door frame,

"Text him the address. I want a word with the serpent that thinks he can call my Pixie an ugly whore." If I had panties, they would be soaked; instead, it runs down my thighs, and from the smirk on all the guys' faces, they are aware. Ren pulls me to him and holds my eye as he reels off the address. All the answer he gets is a grunt and then a dial tone.

"I've got to split soon," Paxton says, stepping towards me, his forked tongue flicking out, tasting my arousal in the air,

"But first." Ren spins me against his chest and holds my legs open, so Paxton has clear access to me.

My back arches as he thrusts his shifted tongue inside me. I can feel it twisting and turning, flicking at my G-spot. Ren is playing with my tits, and Trick takes my mouth, Pax tears his mouth from my cunt,

"Open wide, Pixie, I need to ease these before work," he starts to push the tip of one cock in my pussy, and the other is guided into my ass by Rivers' shadows, which are also teasing my clit,

"That'ssssss it, my beautiful Pixxxxxie, our perfect Mate." his words are more hiss than actual words. Trick presses the tip of his cock against my lips, and I open greedily for him, relaxing my throat so he can give anything he wishes.

I would groan out Pax's name as he fills my ass, but Trick fills my mouth, then I scream out Pax's name again as River pinches my clit at the same time Ren sinks his teeth into the mark on my shoulder, setting off my climax. Paxton moans out my name, sending hot spurts of his cum inside me. He slowly pulls out, but I grab him, licking his cocks clean of our releases,

"You're in my bed tonight, Pixie. I love you." I end up in the shower filled between Ren and River,

"So full", I gasp out before River's shadows fill my mouth,

"You will never be full enough, baby," Ren growls out against my neck.

"Fuck, firefly, your tits look amazing. Next time, I want them painted in my cum." Ren strokes a hand over my stomach.

"Soon, this will be filled with our pups, and when this is swollen, and your tits get heavier, none of us will be able to keep our hands off you." I can feel him getting harder inside me,

"Fuck the thought of her breasts getting bigger and leaking milk for our babies, fuck Quinny, make them cum so I can have you again." I start to lose sense of time, and soon I'm sitting on the sink unit with Trick pounding into me, I remember going back in the shower and one of the guys cleaning me, but not much else.

I wake to a note on the pillow next to me.

Rest, Baby, we got our home today, love you x

I have no idea what he means, as we agreed to leave the place for a week to give Jake and Lia time. I roll out of bed and wince. I need to sort that out if I'm in Paxton's bed tonight,

ME: Need your brand of healing,
I will be in your shower if
You are willing x

I send Creed a text as I walk naked to his room. Cum still dripping from me even with the showers, I have just finished washing my hair when Creed steps in before I have a chance to speak. He pushes me against the wall and slams into me.

"Creed", I moan out and then gasp, tears prickling my eyes. With my soreness, he pounds into me then, pulls out as he cums, then rubs his cum into my skin, rinses himself off, and leaves. My eyes fill with tears as I finish my shower. He's lying on his bed.

"You're angry?" I ask, but he doesn't look at me, and the tears start to fall down my cheeks as I release what I've done again, "I'm sorry." I turn to leave the room.

CHAPTER TWENTY– TWO

CREED

I notice tears fill my precious mate's eyes as she tells me she's sorry, turning to leave my room. I slide off my bed and sink to my knees before her.

"I'm not angry with you, babe. I swear, I would tell you if you made me feel used. I love you, Smudge, so much, I'm angrier with them for leaving you hurting." I slip my tongue into her pussy, and when her thighs start to shake, I move her to my bed, her whimpering with need at being denied again.

"I wasn't hurt, I had an amazing ache if a little stiff, but Paxton asked for a night, and I've only had one proper one with him and Saint." I hum against her clit,

"Then I want a night just me and you soon as I normally share." I lap at her clit until she screams her release,

"I love you, Smudge, so much."

EMBER

"You guys are going to make me a slob if you keep wrecking me with orgasms. I'll be sleeping all the time," I mumble against Creed's chest, his hand stroking my back,

"Come on, smudge, let's get some food." Creed chuckles. On cue, my tummy grumbles. Chuckling, he scoops me up and carries me to my room so I can put on more than his t-shirt. I keep his shirt but slip some boxers and leggings on; I don't bother with a bra because sometimes they need to live free. 'I'm not the only one who sighs with relief when I take off my bra, am I? Oh good! It's the same with socks, am I right?'

The guys are all sat around the TV room with the NFL Replays playing quietly with their laptops, I plonk next to Kodi and Creed plops a plate of sandwiches, chips and a bowl of fruit next to me, ooo fresh melon and strawberries yes please, mumbling a thanks to Creed around a mouth full of melon, I frown at Kodi's screen, he's shopping.

"What are you guys doing?" I frown again when Kodi takes something out of his basket and puts a cheaper version in,

"We don't want you paying for everything as we have all been saving for a while, so we are kitting out our own bedrooms and offices or workrooms," Jace informs me with a stern look,

"I've already ordered the gym equipment and some stuff for Kodi's workshop and Paxton's Garage. Before library stuff is ordered, we need to go through what I still have in storage. Miles has a list of Furniture that I kept of Elise's, but as far as I'm concerned, that money is pack money, just not in name to protect it like the pack lands are." They all give me various looks that I don't want to dig into too much right now.

I shrug, the money will only sit in the account if it's not used, I've only been using the monthly interest so far, and I'm not making a dent in it, but I wonder if the guys don't realise that,

"Let us do this, baby, soothe our male egos a little, use your money for the foundations you want to set up, I know you want to foster kids too, and I'm happy with that alongside our own babies," Ren says softly, I give him a small smile, the few times we have had a night alone we have discussed the future and our plans,

"Eat Angel, it makes my bear nervous when he thinks you're hurt, sad, tired, hungry or stressed." he seems shy about voicing this, so I rest my head on Kodi's shoulder as I munch.

"It's a bear trait, Bas is a nightmare if we get ill or when Dec comes home injured. I learned quickly not to tell him I couldn't feel my wolves when you needed them." Bray chuckles at the memories,

"Probably would have been worse if he had realised it was because you were hurting at the time," Bray mumbles, wincing at the thought.

Miles chirps up every now and then for votes for things in public areas, but he's assured me that he is using the card I gave him. I start making a note of things we want for outside in the future, but better to have an idea of where they will be placed. A kids' play area would be cool.

"As kids are a big plan for the future, what did you all do for school? I know Uncle Nic is the headmaster at the Human High School, but until then, you don't have full control of your shifts." I look at my Twin.

"We were homeschooled and then headed to high school if we had control of our shifts." I nod, then grab an empty pad. Two hours and lots of lists later, I message Uncle Nic, Uncle Luc, Nate, Liam, Alma and the oldies to meet me in Dad's office. I step in, and they give me a curious look.

"First off, I'm not pregnant, so don't panic," Trunk bursts out laughing, and Pops strolls in and double-takes at my words,

"This is purely an idea, but it may affect and benefit your pack and ours." At their nod, I take a seat in Dad's chair. I hear a click and realise Alma just took a photo of me, she sticks her tongue out at me and gestures for me to continue,

"Bray told me they were all home-schooled until high school, if Lia, Lily, Bas, Vicki, Timber and I, along with the few females already knocking out kids at the same time, that's a lot of people doing individual homeschooling." I place a map I drew of the area with the two pack lands and the land I know Liam owns on the desk, I point to a section.

"Right here is a patch of land that links our three areas and is clear, if we were to build a school there that the three areas could use, and put up housing for teachers like Liam, Nate and Lily that have to move regularly because humans notice they are not ageing could live on pack lands and not worry.

We could also offer housing to more teenagers and have an orphanage set up, have like dorms with a kitchenette and an adult on that floor to keep an eye on and help fewer kids like me and Trick who get lost in the system. I plan to set up a foundation to help those ageing out get further education. We could offer them a scholarship or accommodation, and they take on an apprenticeship at the sawmill, with the construction or landscaping companies," I notice Liam and Nate making notes,

"If we see if Mickey G has a trusted social worker, even one that by human standards is close to retirement, that could work in-house and a psychologist, we could form our own group home.

How many widowed or pack members are there who can't have children but would help a child? Hybrids like Bram are regularly dismissed because no one wants to deal with the uncertainty of their abilities. I've talked to Ren about setting up some foundations, but why not start with this? It will help us, both packs are preparing for when we start having kids, Miles could have omegas, and the safest place would be pack lands." They all just stare at me.

"Why didn't we think of this sooner?" Uncle Nic runs a hand over his face,

"We have 16? 18? 20? boys living with us, they could have all had individual mates with our nephews and niece; they are all likely to have multiple births, as it's in the family. We also have 2 more sets of twins." At Luc's words, his eyes widen at me, realising I'm a twin mated to two sets of twins. Alma perks up,

"Liam, Nate, do you know any teachers or psychologists who

would be interested in teaching young supernaturals? We could probably do with another doctor and nurse, too, or we are going to burn poor Xander out." Following her line of thinking, Liam nods

"He has already mentioned getting a midwife. I know you and another lady are trained, but as I said, we have the potential for a lot of babies coming soon" Liam and Nate share a look.

"We might be able to help there; we have a few friends who could, to be honest. But regarding running it we have a friend who is a sun bear but she was mated to an Angel before he was killed so she has his eternal life span her name is Mirri Flowers." after a few moments and a nod from most of us, he steps out to call her, Uncle Nic texts Mickey G, and the fax sets off as Liam steps back in,

"She says she can visit next week for a few days, but if she takes the job, her adopted daughter would have to come too, she is training to be a midwife."

Alma decides to sort out one of the guest cabins out and Trunk says he will oversee the site and has a team that is normally on backup, as most are retired. We spend some time going over what buildings we need and the size, depending on capacity and how many staff we will need.

CHAPTER TWENTY-THREE

EMBER

Lia messaged last night to say it was safe for workers to come back to the site, so work started again this morning. Dad and Lily wandered in during lunch. Lily gave me the list of sketches she likes and asked for a couple of tweaks. Now that I've finished Declan's Birthday gift, I plan to start on her commission. We agreed I would do canvases for her big one, but they will then be jig-sawed together, so it's not one Giant canvas we need to move. Trent appears

"There is someone called Swift at the gate for you?" I glance at him and then frown at the clock,

"Are Ren and the guys still sparing outside?" he nods.

"Bring Razor to them, please, but make it clear no one is happy he is late, he said tomorrow, and that was nearly a week ago." I smile at Trent, and he chuckles, dashing off,

ME: Are you home? Swift has finally turned up x

PAX: Yeah, was about to have a shower but will head down now x

I step outside, and Uncle Luc smiles and hooks his arm around my shoulder.

"Guys, carry on, but Swift has finally decided to turn up", I state as Pax joins us, my phone dings.

LIAM: Mirri is coming to dinner, I've already messaged Alma. :)

I don't have a chance to reply as Uncle Nic and Dad join us, Trent rounds the corner with Razor Swiftly, swaggering slightly behind.

Ren is currently sparring with Bram and River, but all three are watching the newcomer, not that you can tell that their focus isn't fully on their match.

"So, which one are you fucking? And which is my room?" I glance at him,

"You're a week late." Trent moves to Miles' side,

"This is the TripleMoon Pack Alpha, Domanic Ivanova, his Beta, Lucian and their older Brother, Makyal, who is also my father," he snorts at me,

"Yeah, don't care, only where the hot girls are, my dick needs sucking." Ren stops the match and walks over. I hand him a towel as he kisses my temple.

"No fucking way, are you shagging Decimus Fall?" Swift blurts out, and everyone freezes,

"Dude, you can do better than this, heifer. You had that hot blonde succubus riding you during the last meet." Ren kisses my lips, then pulls the collar of my t-shirt out of the way and kisses his alpha mark.

"Even if you were a friend and you addressed Decimus in such a way, your throat would be torn out." Ren stands to his full height, pulling his shoulders back,

"You are very lucky I am not my half-brother." Ren's voice pulses with Alpha Command.

"However, you are being rude to the Pack Alphas, their niece, and my Luna, the last person who called her a whore in my presence died with my teeth, tearing out his jugular." I shiver at the memory, but my core clenches and I feel my panties get moist.

"Razor Swiftly, I would like to introduce you to Alpha Ren Firefall."

Ren snorts at the shocked look on Swift's face, and Pax steps forward

"You're the one who thinks our mate owes you something?"

Swift steps back a little. As a snake shifter, he can shift into various types of snakes. At his retreat, I would guess a basilisk isn't one of them in his arsenal.

"Yeah, she only passed that class with my help, so she at least owes me a room for a few months," he's turned cocky as hell.

"I looked it up. You flunked the class and only turned up 25% of the time, whereas Ember had 100% attendance and passed with honours, so how did you carry her and not pass yourself?" Darby says, spinning the tablet around to show the results, he opens something else, and whatever it shows makes Pax shift, freezing Swift in his gaze. He turns, and his huge snake head bumps against mine. I kiss his head, then he shifts back,

"Love you, Pixie."

"Love you too." I smile at him as Saint and Dec appear,

"Razor Lorane Swiftly, you are under arrest for a large list, which we will discuss after Paxton's Gaze wears off." Dec places cuffs on Swift before they disappear into the shadows again.

Dinner that night was fun. Mirri likes all my ideas for the school. She spoke quickly to her daughter and then decided to rent one of the cabins from my uncle, so they were here for the setup of the school. The oldies don't seem happy, but I think that's because she and Alma bonded; they are not yet outnumbered, so they are just acting weary when the two women are around. I am sleeping in Kodi's room tonight. He is still nervous about hurting me, so we have soft kisses and hugs, but I love every second of it.

I message Vicki the next day to confirm the details for Dec's birthday party, Bas, Bray and I decided to do a kid's party theme, with party games and fancy dress, her heat broke two days ago so thankfully she's up for it, after texting back and forth a few times she decided on an outfit and she's looking forward to trying out ALL the games.

DECLAN

I know I'm moping as Victoria hasn't made it here yet, even though her heat was over, I just got 'I'm busy' as a reply, and everyone else seems to have forgotten it's my birthday. I'm just getting back from picking up Ember's order from the art shop that she needs to do the commission for Lily when my phone dings,

> **BABY SIS: Need help on the deck,**
> **I will help you empty the truck in a bit. X**

I huff and trudge through the house as I step onto the deck. I double-take, there are Thomas the Tank Engine balloons, streamers and banners everywhere. Everyone is in retro '90s clothes, Bray has those ridiculous curtain bangs going that I know I sported at some point, Victoria is there smiling at me wearing trackies with poppers up the sides, a girl power boob-tube, platform sandals and her hair in Britney Spears pompom bunches.

Out of nowhere, my baby sister jumps on my back,

"Happy Birthday, big brother, we got cake, pass the parcel, balloons, cake, musical chairs, Karaoke, cake, erm, you got presents, and there's cake" She's talking a mile a minute and when I manage to de-tangle myself from her, she's dressed in a rainbow tutu that seems to be shedding glitter, leg-warmers, and I heart Backstreet boys t-shirt, her hair is in high crocked pigtails and she has an odd hair band on that has pompoms on springs.

"You need to go get changed, then come party, go, go, go, go, go."

I glance at Saint for help,

"You said you missed certain stuff with her not growing up here, so she decided to remind you why you're lucky you missed some stuff. Good luck getting that glitter off anything it touches," he pats my shoulder.

I run upstairs to get changed, hoping Miles has left me something, which he has, baggy trousers with the crotch at my knees and a Post-it note, 'can't touch this'. I laugh out loud, an Nsync t-shirt and some high-tops, a pot of hair gel and a photo of what I'm expected to do.

I step into my bathroom and spike my hair up, washing the gunk off my hands. The wall opposite my bathroom door is normally covered in photo frames, but unlike normal, most are covered in tissue paper, and there are a few on the sides too. The one that should hold a photo of Bas and me with a newborn Bray has a tag hanging from it.

> Big Brother, I hope the switch is ok, the old photos are behind the new, I just thought some needed a little more. – I love you x

I pull the tissue paper away, and there is a coloured sketch of Bas holding Bray and me holding a baby with fuzzy red hair.

The next one I uncovered was the first time Bray walked. Now it shows the original with Bray walking between Bas and me, but Ember is lying on the floor sucking her toes, a post stuck to the frame.

> Why walk when I have brothers to carry me?

I know I have tears falling, but I still laugh at her logic.

There are some of the birthdays and a few at pack meets, first days at school, she changed my graduation photo to have her and Bray behind me posed with Grumps, and the twins are pulling faces at the camera, there are photos of me, Saint, Paxton and Layton passed out drunk with Grumps expensive booze and her drawing on our faces, her tongue sticking out in concentration, I know the original photo was taken by Bray so I know his part in it.

There are three new ones on my dresser, and when I uncover them they are new photos, not sketches, of the four of us, one around the firepit, one at dads mating ceremony and another of us playing Xbox in the TV room, there is another on my bedside table, and it's a sketch from Ember's college graduation of us all. Before I leave the room I notice a large piece on my desk, and when I pull the tissue off its of us all in our shifted forms, Ember sat on the floor reading a book, me standing behind her eyes glowing red, fangs peeking between my lips, Bas in full shift to our right and both of Bray's wolves to our left, the background is the TripleMoon lands and crossing in front of a crescent moon is a phoenix.

Wiping my face as I descend the stairs, I go straight to my sister, pulling her into a hug.

"Thank you."

I hug her tight, knowing I'm crying, but I don't care. It doesn't take long for Bas and Bray to join the hug, and I can hear some fucker taking photos, but again, I don't care; my sister is home, and we are all together, and we are all safe.
"We are all doomed to be covered in this glitter until we are older than Liam," Bray grumbles, making us all laugh.

"Well unless I'm right and there is something in the water that will make me a Barbie Bitch, you are lucky I'm not a girly girl, BUT one day you will have nieces and there is Miles around who will influence, so Yeah, we are screwed" Ember chuckles as she heads over to Miles rubbing against him then runs away giggling.

I can't wait for the future she makes me picture.

CHAPTER TWENTY FOUR

MAKAYL

This year is definitely better; all four of my kids are trying to win a game of musical statues against the oldies, who are claiming they are not cheating by sitting down to dance. My father has never smiled as much as he has with my baby girl around. Lilliana finally agreed to fully bond with me. My kids are happy and finding their forevers.

I know Bastille is ready, but I'm glad it's not hitting us all at once, or some celebrations will be lost in the mayhem. I watch as Lily wanders to each of my children and then heads inside. I decide to follow when I notice my children are following her like little ducks,

"I know I'm doing this an odd way, but it's the way that feels right." Lily pushes me, so I'm sitting, and I see Ember push the three boys down, all three glaring at her. She just turns and looks at Lily.

"I found out this morning that I'm pregnant" Silence, I can't even hear breathing,

"I'm around three months." Again, no one moves, no one breaths,

"DAD," Ember growls at me,

"Erm," is my only response, causing my daughter to roll her eyes at me,

"I can't wait, I'm going to be a big sister" She hugs Lily and then pulls back,

"Single? Twins? Triplets? Quads?" Lily laughs and covers

Ember's mouth.

"Twins and I would like to find out the sex before you start firing off more questions." I finally snap out of my stupor,

"I love you; I am happy, just shocked." I kiss her and hold her close.

"Xander bless him, came to me in a flap, your injection was due the day Ember came home, and in all that excitement, he forgot yours, Luc's and Nic's. He was so apologetic, but we went straight to the clinic and took a test." I kiss her, I don't care,

"We are still going to be the best set of twins." I hear Brayden whisper, and he gets an elbow to the gut from Ember,

"It's not a competition, Bray, let's hope one isn't greedy like you and steals the height, muscles and alters, even though from what Xander found out, it could be genetic." I hear a thump, and then the kids start to bicker. I just hold Lily, and we watch our children fight about who's going to be the best older sibling. I just silently wish nothing goes wrong with these two.

EMBER

Ren and Trick's birthday is in a week. Trick told Alma and me that he just wanted a meal of all his favourites. He doesn't like parties anyway. Ren grumbled the other day that people at school won't stop asking about the upcoming party they expect to happen, and the shifters have got worse, hoping that when he announces his pack at his party, they will be part of it.

He got so pissed at the pack meet the other day, he yelled at some Barbies and told them he was having a quiet meal with his family, he didn't want a party, and his Pack knows who they are already.

Since then, Lia, Alma and I have been working behind the scenes, they will have a meal, but it will be our first pack meal in our new home, it's not finished by any stretch of the imagination, but the Kitchen and dining room is, and we managed to get the beds up in all the bedrooms, Bray's Cabin isn't done so I've set up a temp room in the main house for them, but the other guy's cabins are done, so I have, go-bags packed, and we took them over this morning.

Lia and I are going to do all the cooking for the evening, and Alma is doing a birthday breakfast as the family treat.

While Lia and I were getting stuff set up in the kitchen, the Minx told me she was also expecting, fell on their honeymoon, and she's praising every deity she can think of that it's only one baby. I gave Mirri a quick call asking when they were arriving. We worked out that Lia is nine weeks gone, but with not only her and Lily carrying, but there are also twelve others within the pack. She told me she would call me back and give me a date, and I confirmed her cabin was ready when they were.

Timber told me at dinner last night that my studio was done, so Matt and I are currently packing up the room I used at TripleMoon, the only stuff being left behind is the stuff for the art show, as why move it twice?

Miles finished putting the stuff that needed frames together this morning, just as we are getting the last of my paints and tablets packed, an older enforcer wanders in.

"Miss, the two new females are here. Where do you want them to put?"

He sniffs at me, I stare at him, then just walk past, ignoring him, "Ms Flowers, it's so nice to see you again." Shaking her hand, I spot Trent and Marcus,

"Guys, can you grab the keys to the Blossom house and meet us there?" They just smile and head off,

"Is it far? I don't think I can manage far in the car." Ms Flowers' Daughter, Oriana, states,

"It's actually quicker to walk if you don't mind someone else driving your car." She nods and hands me the keys, which Matt takes,

"I got it, Bas and Timber are loading your studio up now and heading over to the new place," he slides in the car and sets off,

"Follow me, it's not far," I say, taking us around the pack house. They ask what type of pack it is, and I explain a little about my past as they click on that I may be the Alpha's niece, but I didn't grow up here.

I point out the trail that leads up to where the school will be and explain that the fridge is stocked and Alma put on a beef stew in the slow cooker, but if they want to come to the main house, they are welcome. They give thanks but say they want to get settled and to thank Alma for the stew.

The next morning, I am about to head to the new place, but see Bas shift and start barrelling around the lake. I spot the direction he's going in and sprint around the other side towards Oriana and stand in front of her, holding out my hands, deciding it's best to talk to the bear than the man.

"BOU STOP!!!" I yell, and thankfully he does hitting the brakes and doing what I can only describe as a bear cub roll 'you know when baby bears do rolly pollys but end up flopped on their back well imagine that with a 9ft bear,' after rolling back onto his paws he starts yelling at me, but he's still in bear form so it's just whines, yowls and growls,

"Bro, I have no idea what you're saying, but I can guess. Miss Flowers is your mate? Then think about what you were doing! You're huge, and you were charging full speed at her. She's a lot smaller than even me when she shifts, now go home, cool off and then introduce yourself properly, or do I need to get Alma and Lily to have words?" I stand, giving him a stern look with my hands on my hips. He shakes his head and then lollops off, after a cub eye look at Oriana.

I turn, placing my hands on my knees and letting out a huge breath,

"Fuck I didn't know I could run that fast! Those cookies did not enjoy it," I pant out, then stand back up straight,

"I'm sorry about my brother, he's the last of my siblings to find his mate, and I think he got excited, I know he's big and scary, but he is a big gooey bear, he gives the best hugs" she chuckles, waving me off, but I do see the relief in her eyes, my theory was right he had scared her a little, we walk around for a bit avoiding talking directly about Bas, when we get back to her cabin there is a basket on the porch, and a note sticking out I chuckle,

"Do you have a photo?" Her voice is quiet. I scroll through my photos and send her one of the four of us. I then pause,

"Do you have more than one mark?" She nods, so I send her two photos. One is of Timber, Bas, Kodi and Trunk, and I let her know who is who I also sent a photo of Bas and Timber in their shifted form, pushing trees out of the way at my place, and I'm sitting on Bas' back when she shows me her marks I quickly take a photo, turning so she can see what I'm doing I text Kodi

ME: What's your brother's mate mark?
Bas is Oriana Flowers' mate,
But she has two marks, and I have a hunch x

KODI: *PHOTO*
Love you x

The photo shows Bas and Timber holding their shirts up to show their marks. They are younger, so I'm guessing it's when they first got them. I forwarded the photo to Oriana,

"Please tell them both, but ask them to give me time." I nod, then she quickly snips some of her hair, and using some gold cord, twines them together and hands me two bracelets. She sends me a photo of herself dressed up for her graduation; she's in a pretty sundress with flowers woven into her long brown hair.

When I get back to the pack house, I find Bas and Timber on the deck, the former sulking, and Tim is agitated as he doesn't know why.

"She asked for a little time, as she has a bad past, and that's how she came to be with Ms Flowers, but she's safe now and has been for a while." Bas nods,

"She has two marks. I messaged Kodi on a hunch, and I was right, you both share a mate. She asked me to give you both these." I slip the bracelets on their wrists and then send her number and the photo of her and her marks to them,

"Start small. She liked the basket, and you didn't scare her; she was just shocked. She grew up around grizzly bears, and you're a lot bigger." Bas nods but looks less sorry for himself,

"*Thank you, baby sister.*" I nod and head off.

I've done my part; it's now down to them.

CHAPTER TWENTY-FIVE

REN

"Baby. J and I just wanted a quiet meal, not a blindfold and surprises." I know I'm pouting like a child, as Ember takes my hand and shadows cover my skin.

JENSON

Quinny holds my hand, and I trust her; she would never do something we were totally against. As the shadows leave my skin, I speak up,

"Bro, relax. Do you really think Quinny would do something we hate?" I get a grunt in response. I get it, Ren doesn't like surprises, as the few we've had in our lives have been shit. Quinny's hand runs up my spine, and then I feel a tug as she pulls free the knot holding the blindfold in place.

EMBER

"Welcome home and Happy Birthday." I pull the blindfold off to show the food-covered tables we have set up. Ren's jaw drops, J kisses me, then heads straight for the food. Everyone is standing by their chairs, waiting to sit. An empty chair at the head of the table is Ren's.

"Lia and I did all the cooking, minus the cake. I think Alma will fight anyone to the death if they try to make one of her boys' birthday cakes and not her."

I glance at Ren, but he still seems in shock,

"All the bedrooms have beds, and most have usable bathrooms. I brought go bags for everyone with help from Miles, so we can all spend the night."

I reach up on my tiptoes and kiss Ren's Jaw.

"Happy Birthday, Alpha," I whisper. I'm about to head for the empty seat next to Trick when I'm scooped up, Ren walks to his seat, then plonks me in his lap, kissing my temple,

"Dig in, guys. Amelia and our Luna worked hard on this feast. Let's show our appreciation." He starts to fill a plate and then places it in front of me before filling his own. It's been fourteen years, and he still does what he did that first time.

"*I love you*," he whispers into my hair, then takes a stuttered breath, the only sign his emotions are a mess.

We all eat and talk about nothing, as Jake and the Quad clear the table, Lia and I are about to get the dessert sorted, but Ren grabs my hand and stands up,

"Thank you for the gift of an amazing meal and our first as a pack. I know not all are sworn to me, and I don't care. I will file the paperwork tomorrow. All I ask is loyalty to the pack and not to bring harm to those who live here.

My brothers and I were raised by an Alpha who ruled by fear, I never want that, I want pack meetings like this where we are relaxed and just share updates even if it is just that Gus unblocked the toilet after Hugo blocked it, I will work with you to keep us safe, I'm not a dictator, I want us to work together and for no-one to fear coming to me with problems, even if it is the fifth time Lia is coming to me to complain Jenson has eaten a whole jar of brown sugar.... Again!" Everyone chuckles at Ren's words, but a round of here, here sounds around the room.

Jake stands, glancing at his mate and brothers,
"We will swear to you and Ember, as our Alpha and Luna, you have shown how you care not just for your family but those that need help, you have both been supportive in our relationship and our ideas away from the roles we play within the pack, and we want our child and anyone's in the future to grow up seeing and experiencing that kind of love and support." Amelia is wiping her face on her pinny, and I quickly wipe my face before I clear my throat,
"The paperwork was filed two days ago. As of 1 am this morning, this is officially the BloodMoon Pack." I hand Jace the paperwork as Ren pulls me into a searing kiss, making everyone chuckle,
"Put her down, brother. I want my cake." Everyone chuckles at Trick. I can hear the laughter in his voice, which is one of the best things about this.

The rest of the night is filled with plan-making and confirming the details already in process, Jake, Amelia and the quad all pledge to the pack, and then they, like Taylor, James, Callum and Marcus, head to their own homes.
Xander heads back to TripleMoon as he has work tomorrow, we sit for a while, I explain to Bray, Miles, Mateo and Bram that there is a room set up for them as their place isn't ready yet but we don't hold them to staying here with us, but they all say it feels right to be here tonight, all my guys give me searing kisses all telling me good night, Trick dibs tomorrow night which I quickly agree too.
Because of the age of the house, Ren and I have individual rooms, but joining the two is a shared room. It currently has a standard king-size bed, which will go in Ren's room when our Californian King arrives. I step into our joined room, and Ren is looking out of the huge bay window that looks out over the pack lands,

he's taken his shirt and socks off and his Jeans are undone but still on his hips, stepping behind him, I press a kiss between his shoulder blades, or as close as I can with our height difference, I press my forehead to his back and thread my hand to his front, one hand sits just below his ribcage, the other over his heart. He takes one hand from his pockets and places it over mine, keeping it safe over his heart.

"We did it, Ember, we made a safe place for us, my brothers and our children." I feel tears drip onto my arm, and I swallow mine back.

He is always strong for me when I break; it's time for me to be strong. Keeping my hand over his heart, I step around him, going up on my toes, I kiss the underside of his jaw, a few pecks, and he lowers his lips to mine.

"Take me to our bed, Alpha, make love to me in our home." he lifts me, and his jeans drop to the floor as my legs wrap around his hips.

Lying me on the bed before he starts to pull my clothes off me.

CHAPTER TWENTY-SIX

REN

I lay her on the bed, kissing her as I remove each item of clothing, the offending items keeping her skin from my touch. Pine wants me to rut her until she's round with our child, but she asked me to make love to her.

I spend my time kissing every inch of her. I avoid her nipples and her pussy, until she is writhing beneath me, then I suck her nipple into my mouth, her whimpers turn to moans, and I smell how slick she is.

"Poor baby, have I teased you too much?" as I talk, my lips brush down her body,

"You can take a little more. I want you gushing before I fill you, baby."

I brush my lips across her core, inhaling her amazing scent,

"Because once I'm inside you." I run the tip of my tongue over her lips.

"I'm staying there until my knot has fully deflated." I spread her folds with my fingers so I can view my meal. She's pink and flushed, her slick dripping down to her puckered hole.

"You know what that means, don't you, Luna?" I blow against her bud.

"Words, Ember, I'm desperate to taste this dripping pussy, but not until you confirm you know what that means." I nudge her clit with the tip of my nose, making her hips jump.

"Mmmm....Oooooo.....Errrrm! When an Alpha's knot doesn't form at all, it means his mate is carrying his child. If your knot fully deflates, I will be carrying your pup... pups." She's panting and gasping by the end.

"Not mine but ours, Luna, all the best parts of me and all the amazing parts of you," I growl, then bury my tongue in her tight hole. I feast on other than a few small flutterings; I keep her on edge until she whines the words, I'm desperate to hear.

"Please, Alpha, I need you inside me." I chuckle and suck her clit, sending her flying over the edge. I surge up, flicking each nipple with my tongue as I swallow the rest of her moans. When she's nearly down, I notch the weeping blunt tip of my cock at her needy opening.

"Please Alpha I need you it hurts to be so empty" I don't like my Luna in pain but she asked for love not a hard fuck, so slowly inch by inch I sink into her, her back arches and she lets out a low moan, I kiss my bite marks, her gorgeous heaving breasts, I don't stop until my knot is fully inside her, rolling my hips as I'm not given much room to move with her cunt clenching on my knot I repeat my vows to her.

"Mind." Roll,

"Body." Roll,

"Heart." Roll,

"Soul." Roll,

"I'm yours for eternity." Roll,

"I love you, baby." Roll,

"My Luna." Roll,

"My everything." Roll,

"The Ember that keeps my heart burning." She goes to reply, but my knot starts to inflate bigger than it ever has before, and a keening moan starts to leave her throat.

Day to day my knot is an inch thicker than the rest of my dick, from the root, it's about an inch too, it's to announce to any willing females I'm ready to breed, normally it inflates like a balloon to the size of a tennis ball when I'm inside her and takes me three or four orgasms for it to shrink enough to pull out of her, it's also hard like a baseball.

"Fuck, so full." She moans, pressing her face to my chest, and I chuckle

"My knot is inflating to the size of a baby's head at the time of birth, none of my cum will be leaking onto these creamy thighs this time, baby." My voice has gone husky, but I daren't move until it has stopped inflating. I breathe heavily on her ear, as I focus just on us, our hearts beating, our breaths, the way the moonlight across the bed makes her glow.

"Fill me, Alpha, make my body swell with your heir." She rolls her hips against mine, whimpering each time her clit rubs against me, with how sensitive she is. We go slow, kissing and nipping at each other.

We are both going to be covered in love bites by morning. Each time she hits a climax, she sinks her teeth into me just short of breaking the skin, six fucking sets of teeth marks, mark my flesh. When Pine manages to push through, my knot shrinks with each orgasm I have, which makes things easier to move.

"My dripping Luna, full of our Seed, but she needs more," Pine growls into her neck. It's the first time he's taken over my voice, and it feels odd. He starts to pound into her, the headboard smacking against the wall until my knot shrinks enough, I can slip from her body.

EMBER

"NO." I whimper as Ren slips from me,

"Don't cry, baby," he whispers. I hadn't realised I was; he rolls me to my hands and knees.

"I just needed to be deeper inside you" his lips brush his bite as he pushes back inside me.

"Please, Alpha, fuck me so deep", he chuffs against my throat, proving Pine is still close to the surface. He cuffs my throat and pulls me to my knees, my back to his chest, it's always a favourite position with him,

"I would never leave you wanting, my Luna." his other hand goes to my breast as I thread one of mine in his hair, I sink my nails of the other into his muscular ass, pulling him more against me, I can feel the flex of his muscles with each thrust, I've lost count how many times I've fallen apart, I started by leaving bite marks but I lost count when Pine gave me four, or was it seven? Back-to-back. I fist his hair and arch my back as he pinches my nipple,

"Fuck your slick smells so good I can feel it running down my thighs."

pushing me forward to my elbows, my hands are yanked from him, and he hisses as I leave scratches on his ass, and I'm sure some hair was torn out.

"Milk my cock, Luna Baby." His Alpha command comes through, and I'm always capable of ignoring it, but I don't; he pounds into me hard, his balls slapping against my clit again. I lose count of how many times he makes me scream out my release.

I don't remember blacking out, but I wake curled against Ren's chest, I kiss down his sleeping body, taking his cock in my mouth.

"Mmmm Luna? Rest, baby, you're bound to be sore!" he brushes the hair from my face as I pull his cock out of my mouth with a pop, then kiss back up his body,

"I want to ride my Alpha! Would you deny me my needs?" I whisper against his ear, lining him up with my needy core.

"Never, baby, I will deny my mate nothing. I love you, Luna." His hands guide my hips as I sink onto his length,

"Good," I moan, setting a fast pace,

"Now enjoy the view as it will soon change if your knotless cock is anything to go by." His eyes go wide, 'he hadn't noticed?' he shoots up, kissing me,

"Ride me, Ember, but know I will want you more and more the bigger you get." I smirked at his words, four orgasms, a shower, 'yes, some were in there,' and we headed downstairs for breakfast.

Well, after Ren spends half an hour kissing my tummy.

CHAPTER TWENTY-SEVEN

EMBER

Ren and Trick's birthdays are over. The guys focus on their exams, technically we should be in different school years, so Bray and I would be with Bram, but Uncle Nic runs his school Jan – December with two sets of final exams throughout the year.
The first in July with the rest of the country, then another just before Christmas, somehow it works, but even I started getting confused, but as it doesn't bother me right now, I shrug it off and leave the guys to it, also, because Supes can learn quicker than humans, it doesn't cause too many problems.

We have slowly started to move our stuff over and spend weekends there, only having the basics back at TripleMoon, but until I turn eighteen, we can't move into the main house.

Halfway through August, we are sitting having an evening meal, I watch my family chatting among themselves, swapping stories of what has happened in the day, I watch as my dad regularly reaches over giving Lily's little bump a stroke, sometimes he gives me and Bray pained looks as if it's hitting him again how much he missed when mum ran off.
"As we are all together, I thought I would share some news." Ren, Bray and Devin keep shovelling food into their mouths as they presume, I'm talking about an art exhibit I have been asked to join. One thing I have been arguing with Liam about. I wait until Ren fills his mouth again.
"I'm Pregnant," Xander jumps up to help Ren who starts to choke

on his food, Lily thumps Dad on the back, whoops I hadn't noticed he was in the same predicament, Kodi and Bas look like they are trying to work out how to secure me in bubble wrap, Bas has already been put in the dog house once by Lily for hovering so hopefully he is kind of calm, I then feel coolness cover my abdomen, looking down I see a web of Saint and Rivers shadows, I sigh and look at Pops whose got tears in his eyes.

"Can you let the litter know, preferably when they are somewhere they can calm themselves down?" The likelihood I am carrying their future mate is pretty high, so they are potentially going to be worse than my mates and brothers with Operation Protect Ember.

If we go for 9 months, which is a normal human pregnancy, I would be due in April, unfortunately, or fortunately, depending on how you view it, Supe pregnancies range from 6-12 months long, so we will see. Not knowing what effect my oddities will have on my pregnancy has made Xander nervous.

As expected, when the shock wears off, everyone is nervous about it being me, as I can't have any drugs to help with pain when it comes to the birth. Alma, Mirri, Oriana and Jake's Ma are thinking up natural remedies that could help, Ren finally snaps out of the shock once he stops choking, I'm then pulled into his lap, one of his hands over my stomach, he keeps urging me to eat more, and breathing in my scent, the focus and need for his own food now gone.

"I love you, my Luna," He'd whisper regularly in my ear.

He knew I was pregnant because of his knot disappearing, but I think the confirmation via Xander has made it a little more real.

Miles has another heat partway through August, and judging by the reactions his guys have, more babies are joining the family. I kind of hope Dec and Bas keep it in their pants for a while. When Dad voices this at dinner one night, Bas chuckles and says it will be a few years yet, with a bright red Timber nodding next to him. Victoria chirped in that it will be at least five years for them, as that's when her Elder stint will be over, which seems to please everyone.

Alma cracked a joke she was carrying Pops, Trunk and Grumps babies after a wild night which caused a lot of spluttering before the females burst out laughing her reply to the guy's silence as she's not having kids as none of them would cope with mini versions of her awesomeness, Liam and Nate found an interesting patch of the ceiling which had everyone laughing again.

LILLIANA

I step into the Kitchen and thank the goddess. I find Ember and Alma both spin to face me as my waters break,

"Grandpa, *call Dad and Xander and get them here NOW, and find a cleaner to mop this floor.*" Ember's Perfect Russian accent is making an appearance. I'm still amazed at how perfectly she does it.

"I'll clean the floor; I've texted Oriana too." Lia comes in wheeling a mop bucket. Thank the Goddess she and Ember were sorting the charity comforters with Alma today. I can hear Nikoli yelling into his phone as Alma and Ember get me to the downstairs room set up for delivering babies.

It was an office with an en-suite, but between Ember and Oriana, they decided to switch it. The office was never used anyway, and Alma was happy as she was fed up with dusting the boring room.

"Let's get you out of your wet things." Alma peels my wet leggings and panties down my legs, 'modesty really goes out the window during childbirth,' then sits me on the edge of the bed while Ember switches my t-shirt and bra for one of Mika's old button-ups.

"In the bed, Mother dearest, wiggle to the middle." I glare at her,

"Let's see you wiggle when it's your turn, brat." She just smirks at me as she lays a sheet across my legs,

"Feet up to your bottom, Lily," Alma says as she sticks her head under the sheet just as Xander walks in. I feel like I should be embarrassed, but at the same time, a contraction hits,

"How're things looking, Alma?" he asks, smiling at me while setting a case down on the side table as if they are talking about a cake, not my vagina.

"Good, not fully dilated yet, which is also good," Xander nods, then heads towards the bathroom to wash his hands.

"Let's do a quick ultrasound to check that the babies are in the correct position and get heart monitors on." I don't see what happens on the scan as another contraction hits,

"Hold my hand, Mother, but wait until it is Dad's to squeeze hard enough to break it, yeah." Says Ember with comfort and humor in her voice. Once the contraction is over, I chuckle at Ember's words. My contractions come thick and fast, and I don't notice when Ember leaves my side until Mika whispers in my ear.

"Time to push my love, time to meet our babies." His voice is full of emotion as he speaks against the shell of my ear, and I manage to kiss his lips before a more intense contraction hits.

EMBER

I watch as my dad talks Lily through bringing my siblings into this world, Oriana arrives with the bag Lily had prepared for the babies and I start setting everything up on the side next to the changing table, yes there are custom-made swaddle blankets that would make the average human cry at the cost but Primark vest and baby grows in true Lily style, Alma sets a baby bath on the counter the other side of the changing table with warm water in and lays a towel over the table

"One more push, Lily." I turn and watch as Lily reaches down with her free hand and strokes the head of the new life she's bringing into the world, my eyes filling with unshed tears, then she screams and squeezes Dads hand, too busy watching them I don't see Xander guiding the baby out and putting the clamp on the cord but I do see Oriana guide Lilys hand to cut the cord, just as a little scream burst through the room,

"Wow, guys, my little brother has a set of lungs." I chuckle as Alma carries him over to be washed off, then places him on the table so I can dry him. I wrap him in a clean towel and take him over to Lily, placing him against her chest,

"Here we go, Dad, meet baby Luka, don't drop him, we don't need another Brayden, even if he only has one wolf" Dad is crying, but he chuckles.

"I heard that," is yelled through the door and I mouth 'Whoops?' which has us all chuckling.

I swipe Luka back up and head over to get him dressed as Lily starts to yell again, Luka starts to fuss as his sister's cry pierces the room.

I pass Luka to Dad as Alma washes baby number two, then I dry her off, wrap her in a blanket and take her over to Lily.

"It's okay, Luka, Nikita is coming," I whisper. I step back and take a photo of the four of them. While Lily feeds Luka, I quickly get Nikita dressed. She's a Hybrid, both wolf and succubae, and strong on both sides. Then I hand her over to Dad before stepping into the hall, my brothers and Uncles are all sitting on the floor staring at the door, and Grumps has dragged a chair over to join them.

"At 1430 and 1438 on the nineteenth of September, Luka Nathaniel and Nikita Bunica came screaming into our lives, and all four are doing well." I open the photo and turn it so they can see, then, at their demands, I send it to the family chat, which is just us, Dad and Lily. Grumps pulls me into his arms,

"This is the welcome you and Brayden should have had" Thankfully, Xander steps out, which halts the emotions warring in all of us,

"Both babies are feeding, and all is well." He kisses the crown of my head before heading off. There is a tenseness to him, so I ask one of my guys to check on him.

"I'm going for a shower, then some food," I say, my nerves are raw after Grump's words, yes, we should have had this welcome, but I can't think that way. As then would Ren have killed his father? Would he still have ended up here? Too much is linked to how we came into this world.

After we have eaten, Brayden and I carry some food for Lily and Dad and of course have some cuddles, which are cut way too short when Dec and Bas turn up, then again Dec doesn't even get sat down before Grumps stomps in demanding his great-grandbabies, after a few photos I usher the grown-ups out, getting tantrums from Dec and Bas when they try to curl up on the couches. I fall asleep to Kodi peppering kisses on my tummy, humming a lullaby.

CHAPTER TWENTY-EIGHT

EMBER

Amelia follows suit on the twenty-sixth of October and brings a perfect baby girl called Raven into the world. Unfortunately, the labour was brought on through stress as her mother found out about her mating and yelled a lot down the phone. Esmeralda turns up two days later, and Jake goes on the full defensive and won't let her in the cabin. Lucky for us, the guys were at our place. Ren and I then banished her from the pack lands as she didn't request permission to enter them in the first place.

After Liam and Nate got her back to one of their properties, she denounced her association with Amelia, claiming she had no daughter and that she wanted nothing to do with the abomination the imposter gave birth to. To say Jake's mother took offence when she overheard, well, they will never be in the same country, let alone state, again.

My guys all went on guard especially the closer we got to Christmas, Dad disappeared on the twenty-third and turned back up at 10 pm on Christmas Eve and a video of Jameson being handcuffed and then it cut to him being put in a jail cell with no chance of parole, after seeing my old social worker like that I didn't want anything else for Christmas, I was happy with his twenty-five year sentence and then fifteen with a magic cuff that stops him from using his magic plus he's been put on a watch list for life.

SAINT

I watch my gorgeous Starshine mix the batter for her Yorkshire puddings. She's only five months pregnant, but she's already huge, and she should be, as she's carrying Quads. We know she's having at least one of each, but nothing specific, as they won't hold still long enough. Her art show last month was sold out, and she donated every cent to children's charities, not that any of us expected her to keep the money.

"Star, come sit down." I hold out my hand, she smiles and comes to me, I run a hand over her stomach, getting a kick from our babies, Ren announced that we would all be dads, didn't matter on the DNA, as far as he was concerned, we were family, and that's how it should be. As she sinks onto my lap, resting her head on my shoulder, she murmurs,

"I want to have at least one baby with each of you," She looks up at me carefully. I kiss her, trying to show her what her words mean.

"I got my injection last week with your dad, guessed it was someone else's turn, but I don't think any of the guys have renewed theirs," Ren says, leaning against the doorframe, a pleased look in his eyes and a smile on his lips, as he takes in our mate.

"Your babies are kicking me again." Ember chuckles as he dashes over, placing his hand next to mine, a huge smile on his face.

"Bray is going to be jealous, Miles is only getting internal kicks, he won't even tell them if it is multiples or just one, the sneaky omega." Ren starts to pepper kisses over her bump, running his hands over her thighs. I tilt her chin and take her mouth,

"I am walking into the kitchen. Whatever you are doing to my sister needs to stop before you scar my mind further." I chuckle at Declan's words as Ember rolls her eyes and huffs.

Later that night, Ren and I get her back in that position, but with fewer clothes and a bedroom door closing her brothers out. The morning after, I'm woken to my Starshine moaning around my cock as Ren fills her from behind. Who would have thought the two kids locked in a concrete cell, with not much hope of survival, would end up with a perfect family, and an amazing future in view?

BRAYDEN

Our birthday comes, and at our request, not a lot is different from normal. We have a pack meet, but this year the lanterns are so that more children can find their forever homes.

This year is so different from last, Ember was laid up in a hospital bed alone and I was morning her loss, I don't think I've let go of her hand for a few hours needing to remind myself she's here, now we are both mated and expecting babies, tomorrow we are having another pack event but it's our pack so like Ren and J's birthday we are having a big meal in our home, as of tomorrow we will be living there, I think the guys moved everything over today, but I have been attached to my Sister so I wasn't paying attention.

On the fourteenth of March, Miles goes into labour, and Ember ends up kicking us all out of the room, as even Matt was stressing Miles out.

Six hours later, Oriana lets us back in, and after giving Miles kisses and love, my Badass, hugely pregnant sister makes us sit in the three chairs provided,

"Miles somehow managed to get pregnant by more than one of you," she states before approaching me with a lilac blanket,

"Lacey takes after her amazing Auntie with some awesome red fuzz Lacey is claiming is hair, and she is ready for a bottle, Daddy." She passes me the bundle, and I hold my daughter close. Once Ember sets me up with a bottle, she heads off, then returns and hands Bram a pink blanket.

"Bronwen has her Daddy's taste for blood, and her fangs are already in, so be careful unless you want to be the meal." Again, she gets him sorted with a bottle. The milk has a pink tinge, so I'm guessing there is blood mixed in.

"And finally, another Daddy's girl baby, Reyna" She passes Mateo a purple blanket and a bottle. She kisses Miles and then heads out, leaving us to feed the babies and Oriana to float around the room. Once the babies are burped and changed, we settle them in the cot and then curl up in the bed with Miles,

"I love our family so much, but I want to wait for a little before the next litter," Miles says sleepily. We all sigh at his news. I don't think any of us are ready for more,

"We got our jabs when Ren and Dad did. Don't worry, we're covered for your next few heats. Sleep, kitten." I kiss my mate's lips and then fall into a dreamless sleep until we are woken to a trio of hungry cries.

CHAPTER TWENTY-NINE

EMBER

SIBLING GROUP CHAT.

ME: Can you distract the guys?
Please x

> **BAS: For how long? X**
>
> **BAS: Wait, are you ok?**
> **Oriana just dashed off! x**

ME: Yes! Ren and Lily are here
But I need the others distracted,
please x

> **DEC: Saint and I are breaking**
> **Some new trainees, Bas get**
> **Timber to help with the others x**
>
> **BAS: GEEE THANKS x**
>
> **BRAY: On it. Tell Ren to keep me posted,**
> **think Dex and Levi are**
> **coming to help you too x**

Ren took my phone from me, placing it on the side.

"You're okay, baby, we're going to get through this and have four gorgeous pups at the end of it." he kisses my lips, his voice taking on a soft purr.

"*I love you.*"

REN

At 11 am on the twenty-sixth of March, my little boy is placed in my arms, and Ember leans over and kisses his head.
"Hello, Kota. He has a wolf, but he has the mage genetics that skipped Brayden and me." She smiles at him, lifting her chin and asking for a kiss from me.

11:30 am, and another Boy is placed in my arms.
"He's like Brayden, but he has a wolf and a kitsune. Hello, Forest." Again, she kisses his head and then me before I lay him next to his brother.

12:15 pm, and I'm given a daughter, Ember chuckles.
"If your uncle is anything to go by, you are going to keep the litter on their toes when you grow up, aren't you, Beautiful Arya, our perfect, little Kitsune?" She barely brushes her lips on her head before she pushes again, with a scream.

12:22 pm, and our last boy comes into the world, and the Alpha dominance coming off him is stifling. Ember kisses his head, and I place him down with his siblings, and all four instantly settle. It's kind of creepy.
"Dante is going to be stronger than you and more protective of his siblings, if that's possible," Ember says softly, watching them with a sleepy smile on her lips.

I kiss my amazing mate, quickly getting photos of the babies, I fire off a text to Bray from her phone that all is well, and to come back before helping Ember get cleaned up and dressed.
The guys are going to kill me; they have had no warning about this, but it's what Ember wanted, so they are going to have to deal with it.

JENSON

Today has been weird, and then Bray says we are heading to TripleMoon for food. I thought we would be home more since we moved out, but apparently not. I'm not complaining, food is food, but when I step into the dining room, I know something is wrong. My twin looks shattered, and he's nervous.

"Before any of you yell this was Ember's plan." he taps his phone and the TV lights up with a photo of Quinny sitting on the bed with four perfect babies in front of her, the photos start to flick through of Ember with individual babies and then an extra of Embers shocked face as she holds a baby with Purple hair, rocking a nice set of Kitsune ears.

"Well, shit, there's a mini-me with Quinny's female sass, I'm moving back here!" Everyone laughs at my comment, Ren confirms they are all okay and are sleeping, so if we all get food now, we can see them after.

One by one, we head in to say our hellos, goodnights, well done and love you's. I pretend to be distracted, finishing my dessert so I can go last, as I step into the room, Ember is sharing a confused look with my brother. I walk straight to her.

"Hey, Quinny, you did good, glad they look like you and not my ugly twin." I chuckle, then kiss her.

"You want to meet your sidekicks, Trickster?" Quinny smirks at me, and I climb up next to her, doing grabby hands,

"Hit me," I say to my brother, who passes me a dark-haired bundle. The blanket says Forest. I take a sniff, then frown.

"Hey, little guy, are you a little tricksy like me?" I glance at Ren, who nods,

"Yes, he has two forms like Bray, but he has a pup and Kit." Ren passes a growly bundle to Quinny,

"At least we have Bray around to help, Dad said that Bray got stuck halfway between both a few times," Quinny says, smiling before whispering to the bundle,

"It's just Daddy Trick, Forest is fine." I look away from the sleeping Kit in my arms, confused why Quinny would talk normally to a baby who doesn't understand words.

"I take it we have a mini-Ren?" While she chuckles, my twin grumbles.

"Yeah, and Dante will only take food from mommy." He moves Forest from my arms and lays him between mine and Quinny's legs before he places a pretty little girl in my arms, who promptly sneezes.

"So cute." Quinny and I say in unison as Arya's ears change to her Kitsunes,

"Mama said you always did that when you were little, your hair used to change a lot, too." Ren passes me a bottle, I copy Ember's actions, and soon, it's chowing down.

I peek over Quinny to Ren's arms and notice Kota stitched on the blanket, and also notice the flash of red hair,

"Kota has the lost mage genes from my side, but he also has a wolf, none show signs of the Angel, but Xander is going to check their blood," Quinny says quietly, watching me.

"So, you ready to start trying for the next lot?" I wiggle my eyebrows at her, and she knows I'm joking from the eye roll she gives me,

"Let's get me back to normal, yeah? I think Darby's head in shifted form can fit up there right now, and there is definitely an echo." I wince at the description,

"Are you sleeping in here?" she tilts her head for a kiss.

"Please?" at her nod, and Ren's grunt. I help Ren lay the babies in the cot. I found out it's the one Mika bought for Bray, and they just got a new mattress for the new family members.

I don't sleep, and neither does Ren; the memories of losing Mama so suddenly after our sister was born keep us awake. Xander comes in four times to check Ember and the babies' vitals before he just crashes on the couch, showing it's not just us, he's been tense with all the babies born, and I think he always will be.

CHAPTER THIRTY

EMBER

It's been two months since our Babies were born, and we are all nicely in a routine. Creed has taken to sleeping in Darby or Devin's room so he can feed. The only problem caused by me being NO SEX is his feeding there have been many tears from me for being a failure as a mate to him, and he got pissed when I offered to suck him off, he stormed off, and I burst into more tears, later he came back with Darby and Devin and told me they said he could feed from their lust to take some pressure off me and all the guys apologised for not thinking he would need a boost.

Trick said they should have a weekly jack off orgy party, which everyone looked at him weirdly, then he realised what he had said and looked horrified at himself, which set everyone off laughing. The Quad soon found out and now randomly shout jack off orgy party whooooooo.

"Everything is nicely healed and back to normal, I would recommend easing back in slowly on orgy parties yeah," Oriana informs me with a wink and wiggling her eyebrows at me, wiggling her hips as she snaps her gloves off, it took me a little longer to snap back with having four natural births but other than my upset over Creed feeding it's not been a problem.

We head to the kitchen to find Lia who is already pregnant again and she's lining up baby bottles like you would see a barmaid lining up shots, all the babies are here today, Lily had a business meeting she had to be in person for, so with my twin siblings, Miles' three terrors, my four monsters and Lia's innocent Raven it's a mad house here, but I can't wait till they are all on the move.

Jenson decided he's going to be a stay-at-home dad, so he is always around, and so are the oldies, who seem to split depending on where they are needed the most. Oriana helps too, between patients. After she fully mated Bas and Timber two weeks ago, we are already ribbing her that she will be joining the baby boom ranks soon.

I still manage to write and paint every now and then, but it is slow going. I find it hard to leave the babies. Kodi is cornering off and padding a section of my studio as a play area similar to the playpen in Rugrats, but shifter-proof.
Dad has been pushing for us to have our ceremony soon, but I want to be fully bonded to all my mates first, and I know I only have Kodiak left, but I don't want to rush him or us. But I do have a plan for it soon, as my bond with him sometimes feels hollow, not because he doesn't love me or want the bond; I get amazing kisses and snuggles from him, and nothing has changed between us, but I think that's the problem. Nothing has changed. Now I've had the all-clear, I plan to take a step in the right direction, and Creed is going to help whether he likes it or not.

I'm standing in the door to the nursery watching my babies sleep when I feel arms slide around my waist,
"What's wrong, baby? You've been distracted since we got home?"
Ren says against my neck,
"I got the all-clear from Oriana this morning and I'm either going to have two very happy mates or two extremely pissed-off ones." I sigh, closing my eyes and leaning back against my Alpha, my rock
"I'm guessing you mean Creed and Kodi." It's not really a question, not really, as we've talked about this a few times,
"I only think they will be pissed if they think you will be hurt, but I think your plan will work, just voice your feelings and be the strong Luna, I know you are." he tilts my chin, kissing me

deeply, he takes a deep breath, smelling the arousal his kiss has caused.

"Go before I ravish you myself." A rumble vibrating his chest, he smacks my ass and pushes me away, making my core clench even more.

CREED

I step out of another cold shower, and the image of Ember on her knees choking on my cock plagues me. I know she's offered to feed me, but I feel like I'm using her. It's why incubi typically take a mistress while their mate is pregnant, but I won't do that to her.

When I step into my room, I find my perfect mate sitting on my bed wearing nothing but a zip-up hoodie. How do I know you ask, the minx has it unzipped while she sits plucking her nipples and circles her clit,
"Smudge", I groan, my dick already hard.
"I got the all-clear this morning." I lick my lips at her words,
"I need your help. Kodi is the last I need to seal my bond with." The word 'need' sounds pained on her lips. She dips her fingers into her core, dragging out a sticky slick to rub over her clit,
"I want you there to make him feel safe and so that I can stop feeling bad for not feeding you." She stands and moves towards me. I dip my head, wanting to kiss her pink lips, but she presses her slick-covered fingers to my lips. I suck them clean, my eyes rolling at the taste of her finally on my tongue, my towel drops to the floor, and I lift her into my arms, strutting from my room to Kodi's. I kick his door shut and lay her on his bed and bury my face in her cunt, licking, biting and sucking at her. I can feel how needy she is.
"Play with those nipples, smudge while I show you how much I want you still." I know Kodi is watching. I saw him from the corner of my eye at his desk when we came in, but at my words, I heard him move
"Why do you think we don't want you anymore, Angel?" The bed dips with his weight, but she can't answer as I'm tongue fucking her through an orgasm, then I start to nibble her clit, I slip a finger into her and glance at him.
"Sit with your back against the headboard, lose the sweats." I jut my chin in that direction as I add another finger and swat her clit with my other hand,

"You're about to learn how naughty your Angel is," I add a third finger

"She's going to slide that tree branch you call a cock into this slick pussy and ride it until she soars." I push a fourth finger into her as she turns her head to look at his erection that is standing proud, waiting for her. Her eyes flare with heat. After a swallow, she starts to lick her lips.

CHAPTER THIRTY-ONE

EMBER

My head turns to look at Kodi, who has just settled against his headboard, tree branch is an apt term, licking my lips, I roll onto my front, Creed's fingers slipping from me, leaving me empty, he grabs the hoodie, so it pulls off as I move away from him.

"I need to finish stretching you before you try to mount him, smudge. I don't want you hurting when you only got the all-clear this morning."

Creed's head slips between my thighs, his fingers enter me again as he starts to suck on my clit, I lick my lips again and lean forward, holding Kodi's eye, I lick him from root to tip, his head slams with a thud against the board and a tortured moan leaves his lips, I do it again and again, I stick my hair in a loose braid so it wouldn't get in my face, using my core strength I grab Kodi's shaft with one hand and the other fists Creeds hair, I tug Creeds hair as I start to pump Kodi's mast,

"Stop fucking your hand and get me ready to ride this before I lose my patience." I tug again on Creed's hair, making him growl against me as I swallow as much of Kodi's cock as I can into my throat.

"Fuck Angel, fuck." is all I get before he starts sending up prayers to the goddess in Cherokee, I hum his amen with him around his tip in my throat, making his hips buck,

"cum down her throat brother, take some of that tension away before you slide into this perfection" Creed demands before biting my clit making me scream, Creed slips out from beneath me as Kodi fills my mouth with a growl, I leave a trail of saliva as I slide my mouth from him, Creed pulls me up so my back is to his chest, I feel his cock slide through my folds

"You ready to seal your final bond Smudge?" he husks in my ear before lifting me up, he moves forward, and one of Kodi's hands joins Creed's on my hip, then the blunt tip of his huge cock presses against my core, slowly he lowers me down, Creed starts to stroke my clit before I'm fully seated but as Kodi bottoms out Creed leaves my back, I can feel both of us throbbing already, as soon as I'm used to his size I start to move.

KODIAK

She sits with her head pressed to my chest for so long, the only reason I'm not panicking is that Creed doesn't look worried; he's sprawled at the end of my bed, stroking his cock slowly.

My Angel takes a breath, and then her hips start to move, she moans and gasps with each movement, my head falls back with another thud, loving the feel of her around my cock nothing I imagined compares to the actual feel.

I can't believe she took all of me, she's so tiny and I'm anything but, her back arches as she starts to bounce on me, her tits moving in time. Creed makes a noise behind her, but I'm not sparing him a glance when my eyes are glued to her. I slide my hand round to cup her ass, fuck, I can feel it jiggle with each downward bounce, I squeeze and help her speed up,

"Mine," she snarls before lunging forward and sinking her teeth above my heart. Once she licks the mark clean, I lift her, spinning her to face Creed and setting her on her knees.

I shift my teeth and bite into her juicy ass, lapping the mark clean before sinking back into heaven.

"Fuck smudge, you look so fucking good." Creed, compliments pumping his cock in time with my thrusts,

"Suck Creed's cock, Angel, we need to fill your mouth, so you don't scream too loud," I whisper. Once her mouth is over the tip of his cock I start to pound into her.

"I hope you're ready, Angel. None of us wants to wait long before you're pregnant again; you made us all suffer while you were. How perfect you looked carrying our babies, this tight little pussy is going to pay, we all have the image of your swollen belly and plump breasts burned into our memory" I notice Creed's head is tipped back and one hand threaded into her hair,

"Fuck I loved it when you would ride me with your bump and your tits leaking milk, your tits have got bigger too and I can't wait to slide my cock between them, or bend you over and watch your ass jiggle as I pound into you, when you were fucking yourself on Kodi's cock I nearly came watching your ass alone, I don't want to cum down your throat smudge, my cum is going nowhere but that dripping cunt of yours." I feel her clench at his words, she pulls her mouth from him and bites his thigh as she cums around my cock, I follow her with the next thrust holding myself deep inside her, she flops forward and I fall backwards but Creed moves, rolling her onto her back, he pushes my cum back inside her before guiding his cock to fill that perfect hole, he holds his fingers coated in my cum to her lips

"Suck." and she does, arching her back and humming at the taste, he's not in her long before they are both yelling their releases. He grabs his discarded boxers and wedges them between her thighs.

Moving her so she's between us, I flick my light off and curl up with them, falling asleep, both me and my bear fully content for the first time since meeting her. I am sorry I waited so long, yes, but at the same time, this was perfect.

CHAPTER THIRTY-TWO

EMBER

Kodiak wasn't lying when he said it wouldn't be long before I was pregnant again. Over the next few weeks, I was filled with cum as often as they could. Ren, even though he was back on the injection, wasn't missing out on the fun either.

I actually thought they were going to give me a break tonight, but no, first Saint takes me in the shower, leaving me with a plug of shadows so nothing can leak out, after a thorough fuck and kiss, he leaves for his job tonight while I'm still drying off.

Jace then pins me to the sink and rails into me while holding my gaze in the mirror. He turns me and gives me a tender kiss before I'm lifted to sit on the vanity by Trick, who fucks me slowly and deep, his kisses matching his thrusts.

At this rate, I'm going to need another shower. They both kiss my cheek and say goodnight as they're on baby duty tonight.

Darby and Devin pin me between them in the doorway to my closet, both filling my pussy again. I'm given goodnight kisses before they leave. I TRY to put clothes on, but no sooner have I slipped a pair of boxers on than they are torn off, and Kodi is pounding me against the mirror in my closet.

I'd learnt my lesson and just climbed into bed. Paxton is soon sinking both his cocks into my pussy. I've barley come down from his venom running through me when River and Creed fill me and take me slowly laying on our sides, River's shadows filling my ass too, eventually I think I'm allowed to sleep then Ren is there, filling me with his Knot, he makes love to me then presses soft kisses against my face as I fall asleep.

I wake in the morning to Creed licking my clit, Ren still filling me with his Knot, small mercies all that', and Jace is teasing my nipples,

"You guys got to give me a break today, I can't take much more." I whine out, my orgasm hits, and then I feel myself dozing off,

"Sleep, baby, our work is done." Ren rumbles in my ear as he slips from my body. I feel a protective hand over my abdomen.

I wake to the feel of movement on the bed and the smell of Bacon. When I open my eyes, I'm shocked not to find Ren but his smiling twin

"Ren's knot disappeared, so we won't be so full on, sorry we went a bit nutso," Jenson says with a beaming smile.

I take the breakfast from him and dig in, to his upset, I eat the lot, even though there was twice my normal amount. Thankfully, or their nuts would be forfeit, they are true to Trick's words, and they go back to normal. Sex is still a regular thing, but I'm not railed by all ten of them in the matter of a few hours. A month later Xander confirms I'm pregnant and lucky me its only twins I think my vagina is happy with that news too, I manage to get a set of paintings done for Lily as she's expanding her business, but I needed to get Liam to finish two for me as I was put on bed rest half way through my pregnancy, at five months I give birth to two boys and it explains why I may have been ill, Harley is a miniature version of Paxton and Basilisk are born in shifted form 'yay no pushing' and Bishop came out not only with a miniature mimic of Saints scowl but also he came out in shadow form 'again no pushing needed' but they think there is a possibility that Harley may have bitten me from inside and it was my reaction to the venom.

Lia has also had her second child, a little boy called Phoenix. All the eldest ones are keeping us on our toes and are getting an A + with their shifting abilities. I had to break out Dan's books on Nightmare and Basilisk babies, as none of the guys knew much about kids. Bishop has a rune anklet to stop him from shadow travelling to Saint. happened once when he needed a nappy change and Saint was in the middle of a mission, my dad, of course, found it hysterical 'Well, once they'd confirmed he was okay,' Declan wasn't as amused as the others.

Dad finally got his wish and we have our Alpha blessing, again Grumps demands he's the one to do the blessing just as he did with Dad, Dec, Bas and Bray's matings, it's a pack affair with a few from TripleMoon but only those we like, including a surprise visitor, Kodi's uncle turned up for a visit and was pointed in our direction after he was introduced to everyone.

I pulled him aside and thanked him for saving my life. He had no clue what I meant until I handed him a copy of the photo of younger him holding a newborn little girl wrapped in a spare jumper. Ashki Usdi Yona Hania Treefall promptly burst into tears.
"What's wrong, little Ash?" Trunk looks confused until he sees the photo, kisses my crown and then directs Ash to sit with Bas and Timber. Turns out he knew more than he thought about me, as after one of the firehouse charity days, he read a book that was left over from the donations, and it was mine.
Bas confirmed most was close to truth but some I down played, after a round of apologies to my Dad, me and my brothers for not calling them about the baby he admitted he had a bad feeling about Jameson but had nothing he could argue with to keep me till Mickey G was available, we all agreed that I had to go through what I did to be the person I am today and be with the people I am so all was forgiven, not that I felt anything I went through was his fault.

The school and group home are now up and running, with the money from Dan and Elise. We have a scholarship program available, but they have to get decent grades and stay out of trouble to qualify. We aren't handing it out like candy.

The guys thankfully gave me a bit of a break after the second pregnancy, not sure if it was from me being ill with Bishop and

Harley or with the older ones causing a few shifting problems. The morning of Dante, Arya, Forest and Kotas fifth birthday I found I was pregnant again, thankfully I'm not too ill this time as with twenty kids running around and thanks to Jenson they are all buzzing on cotton candy, thankfully the litter are good at keeping Arya out of mischief, they are great with all the kids, Ren was worried they would show favouritism to Arya but like today they turned up with 4 custom made mini dirt bikes, each painted to match the personality of each of the kids, Pops was not impressed but once he saw the kids with helmets and padded like the stay puff marshmallow man he was soon giving them tips on how to do tricks, and also insisted they learn how to care for the bikes themselves.

Our pack is getting bigger Callum, Marcus and James all found their mates, Marcus first in one of the female cleaners we took on, due to the type of pack she came from they waited eight months before they bonded and he was always leaving gifts and surprises for her, James found one of his in our group home, Billy was about to age out and came onto pack lands to ask the Quad if he could have an apprenticeship with them, he took Marcus' old room until theirs was built.

Shortly after they started building the cabin, the other arrived with Saint and Dec. They turned up with a human who was in one of the facilities they were shutting down. After Xander patched her up, she asked if she could stay; she had no family, so no one to return to.

Lia started teaching her to make herbal soaps and creams, and with a chance meeting one day, her fate was sealed with Marcus and Billy. Well, after Lia and I explained what it was, she was feeling and why it was so instant, they had a private ceremony just them, Marcus Callum and Trent, with me and Ren doing the blessing.

Callum is another who found his mate through the group home. Nat came with a baby in tow; she was an unlucky one and had a really bad placement. Her human foster brother took advantage.

Callum actually had a soft spot for Baby Hugo before he met Nat. Not only did he ask for her hand, but he also asked to legally adopt Hugo. I'm still unsure if Nat knows, but baby Hugo's sperm donor will never violate a female again. Personally, I'm surprised he will be able to walk again after some therapy.

Xander also met his mate in Ignatious's assistant, Jimmy. Jimmy is a little clumsy and fell down three flights of stone stairs at Ignatious' office, and he called Xander to help. I think Xander's place was stripped of sharp edges by the time Jimmy moved in, and after a little whoops, Jimmy is now banned from the medical area.

Trent hasn't found his mate and I regularly find him rubbing over his heart where I suspect his mark is, Cin took him for a walk a few weeks ago and things have been better since he explained it could be his mate hadn't been born yet and he has an Arya somewhere in his future, other than a comment of maybe someone less troublesome please he has been okay.

CHAPTER THIRTY-THREE

JACE

On Christmas Eve, Ember's waters broke thankfully for the second and this birth we weren't all kept in the dark and knew what was going on. We all decided to let Ren be with her for all the births; his Alpha instincts were going to be the worst to control, not knowing if she was okay. Three hours after they went into the room, Ren exits and hands a little boy to Darby, "Ember picked Ryuu as a name." Darby nods, but from the tears in his eyes, I'm guessing he doesn't trust himself to speak. Ren then hands a lilac bundle to River.

"Hello little Melody" he mumbles sinking into a chair next to where I'm sitting, slipping an anklet on the baby like we had to with Bishop, Ren dips back into the room and then comes out with two more bundles passing one to me and then the other, I feel Creed step behind me and gaze down at the nearly identical girls, the only difference is the hair colour one has my blonde hair the other Embers fiery red hair, they have letters on their blankets,

"Meet Mia," he strokes a blonde head,

"And Lexie," he strokes a red-covered head,

"You guys can go back in. Ember has changed, and we're ready to sleep"

The birthing room is set up with a main bed and some fold out beds, and a few hospital cots, Miles always calls them fish tanks, but we invested after Harley was born in his alter form, after we feed the babies and set them in their tanks, we all give our amazing mate kisses, I slip into bed with her and hold her until our babies wake demanding to be fed and changed, then we switch who has snuggles with Ember, there are a lot of 'love yous' on our lips each time we fall asleep.

EMBER

Six months after Ryuu, Melody, Mia and Lexie are born. The police turn up at our door looking for me. River leaves in an instant to grab Ignatious, which the two officers are not happy with when he walks in, seems Jameson, my asshole of a social worker, isn't done interfering, and I have to appear in court, why I needed armed officers instead of a letter is beyond me. The fact that Ignatious barely held in his hysterics when he noticed Ren and Dante in matching stances with their arms crossed and scowls firmly in place, he even snapped a photo of them while the police were still present, and I will admit Dante is so cute when he goes all Grumpy Alpha.

The morning of the court case, I found out I was yet again pregnant. The guys have been getting the injection as soon as they find out which of them is the baby daddy of the hour. This time I'm thankful it's a single baby, so hopefully an easy run.

Miles dressed me in dark grey wide-legged trousers, grey Converse and a navy off-the-shoulder t-shirt. My hair was half up, half down with the slide Kodi made for me, and I had a navy/gray crochet wrap/shawl type thing in case I got cold.

Ignatious and Jimmy bracketed me as I looked around. I noticed not one human, which I let Ignatious be aware of, and that seemed to make him nervous.

It is an open court so there are spectators in the docks here for whatever entertainment came from the day cases, none of the people I recognised, as Jameson enters I noticed a very young succubus who was dressed like a romance novel receptionist, ruby red lace bra and all, there was also an older male vampire who looked rather smug, I noticed a few of the jury shuffle and then glance back at Jameson and his lawyers.

"The female is sending out influence, I can tell it's hitting the Jury, but not if it's affecting anyone else," I whisper to Jimmy, knowing Ignatious will hear too. I also notice the guard in front of me tenses and glances at the Female.

"Your honour, I would like for Mr Porter's assistant to either stop trying to influence the room or be dismissed from the room." Ignatious voice Booms through the room. The Judge, an elderly dragon/incubus hybrid, looks up from the file before him and nods,

"Miss you either put on a magic cuff or leave if you can't be trusted, Mr Porter, you know better in my court! Cover yourself while you're at it. This is a courtroom, not a second-rate porn scene." his voice sounds bored, but I can tell by his gaze that it wouldn't take much for him to throw them out. I can feel Jameson watching me, but I'm frozen as a female nightmare appears behind the Judge, accompanied by Saint

SAINT

I'm livid when I realise it's Ember's case we were requested to 'help' show the true past; I step to the judge's side.

"Your honour, the Female is my mate; do you wish me to leave?" I've used my shadows to hide my voice from all others, but he shakes his head, the female to my side keeps brushing against me and its pissing me off, at our mating ceremony Ember gifted us with rings like humans have to show her claim even to humans, I made sure this woman had seen it but she wasn't taking the hint, I notice Ember say something to Ignatious and he nods.

"Do either you, Ms Ashes or Mr Jameson recognise any of the Jury?"

Jameson is quick to answer.

"No, your honour." LIE.

Ember stands and gets another nod from Ignatious.

"Not on the jury, your honour, but the handsome dark angel behind you is one of my mates," she says with a small smile. The Judge chuckles, and I feel the female at my side tense and her powers crackle with anger.

"Agent Knight has informed me of that, so I have no objection to him staying and doing the job requested of him." I see Ember relax a little, Jameson's lip curls at the information, and he whispers to his lawyer.

CHAPTER THIRTY-FOUR

EMBER

Jameson has gone from accusing me of being a worthless human with the knowledge of the supernatural to being a powerful mage who has manipulated thousands of people, I step forward so Saint and Lilith 'apt name for the sour bitch' can use their shadows to show the Jury my memories of Jameson, thankfully Saint has been working with me for years to hide my sight and show it as an aura in my memories, I can tell straight away Lilith doesn't like me, she slams her shadows into me but I know Saint will keep me safe so no mental walls are stopping her and she physically stumbles. "Ms Ashes, can you show us your memories of Samuel Jameson, please?" the judge asks, so I start at the earliest one.

"Shut your mouth and stay hidden. No one wants a worthless brat like you; only your cunt is worth anything," Jameson sneers at me as he pushes me into the broom closet. I watch through the slats, and I notice my dad walking in,

But I don't recall that part of the memory, I was busy trying to work out what a cunt was and why it would be useful.
"Ms Ashes, how old are you in this memory?" Saint squeezes my hand
"I was three, your honour, I forgot about the man. I was too busy trying to understand Jameson's words, the man is my biological father, Alpha Makyal Ivanova"

We watch as Dad asks if there are ANY three-year-old females in the home, and every person denies my existence.

The memories continue, being taken from Ren with cloth pressing against my nose, being thrown to the Hounds, leaving me at the Den, the zigzag drives where he would eat and leave me hungry, I show the snip bits of the cage even though it's just him being mentioned, I show my time at the pit and how I ended up with the Lennox pack, I finally end with him trying to convince my real family that they were mistaken, as the memories fade Saint kisses my forehead,

"Any questions?" the judge asks, a snarky voice perks up

"How come you didn't speak up when your apparent father was asking for you, even stating your date of birth?" I look towards the crystal mage

"I was a three year old, told to shut my mouth trying to work out what a cunt was, I am not a shifter I was regularly told I'm a worthless human with only the knowledge of the supernatural, I can tell what people are from their auras and once Jameson found that out he had me tested, multiple times human, wolf and mage in various combinations came back, my subconscious recalls those facts but how many three year olds can concentrate on more than one thing, plus at that group home I was fed one slice of cold toast for breakfast with a glass of tap water, no lunch just some more water and evening meal was what was left after all the other shifters had eaten and a mug of warm weak tea no milk, I was hungry, wearing a dress that didn't fit and no shoes I would guess but I don't remember that I didn't have underwear. So you tell me, why didn't I call out?" She just sniffs at me as a few of the other jurors make noises in agreement with my statement,

"Ms Ashes, why did you never ask teachers for help? Or police? Other social workers?" I look at the Man who asks, he's a raccoon shifter. I look at Saint.

"Can you show them, please?" he nods and takes my hands again the images flow from me, me telling someone then I would be moved to a new location, or a suicide notice would appear in the papers, the PE teacher that reported I had suspicious bruises and I seemed underfed, was investigated and then ended up in prison for child abuse allegations which he pled innocent of, he was raped and killed within the first week,

"I understand now, Ms Ashes" Saint stops the real, and I notice a few of the jurors look a little green. With no more questions, I retake my seat

"Mr Jameson, please step forward. If you have never done this before, it is easier if you let them in than if you resist" Jameson is tense and he cries out in pain, his knee wobbles with the pressure

"Mr Jameson can you show us your memories of Ms Ember Ashes, starting when you collected her from the firehouse please" I watch Saint get more and more angry, Ignatious and Jimmy can see but I opted not to, not needing new memories to dream about, as they finish Saint gives me a nod and I feel the brush of his shadows on my cheek and tummy before he storms out,

"Any questions?" the judge asks, ignoring Saint's actions, ten hands raise.

"Why, when you received the call from your colleague, Giovanni Michaels, did you lie about Ms Ashes' date of birth and parentage?" is asked.
"She wasn't a shifter, so it didn't seem pertinent."

"Why was she always hidden away at the first group home?" is another question I have always wondered.
"She appeared human so that others didn't miss out on permanent homes, because others felt curious, it was easier and quicker", he shrugs, looking bored.

"Why did you try to get her back once she found her family?" he blinks and takes a moment to reply.
"She was still a minor and ran from her mate. I was trying to return her."

"Why did you remove her from kind homes and place her in unsafe ones? You claim she is human, why not put her with a human family?"

"She's aware of the supernatural, if she let slip it could cause problems, hence why she was kept with our kind", this is sneered at the lady who asked.

"Why move her so often and have so many tests done?"
"The families grew tired of her antics", Jameson snaps,

"You are tasked with caring for our misplaced and forgotten young. Why place them in these horrid places instead of reporting those places?" Jameson just shrugged at this.

"How did you keep what was happening from your supervisor? surely he or she would notice one child moving so often," I chuckle at that one.
"I can answer that one, my files were kept on paper, not in the universal system, and his direct supervisor is his step-dad, they just don't advertise that information" There are a few gasps, and the Judge scribbles something down. Jameson snarls at me, demanding how I know that information, and I just give him a smirk.

He never realised I had shifter senses, so I could listen to his hushed conversations when he called his mummy,
"Why do Ms Ashes' official records state she was adopted at a few months old, but not by whom?" The guy points to a printed form, which is then shown on the TV screen.
"A family did, but they died in a car accident, I must have forgotten to change the records", another bored shrug.

"Why was Ms Ashes' file never made digital? Or given the DNA testing, ALL children in the system are required to do?" The guy who asks is smug,
"The DNA came back different each time, and where she was upsetting families so often, I used the spare time I should have been typing her file up, carting her around."

The last to ask shakes her head at Jameson and turns to me,
"Ms Ashes, how did you survive?" I smile.

"I had some kind friends along the way, plus Nikoli Ivanova is my grandfather, and his stubborn Russian blood pumps through my veins" I hear the judge chuckle at my answer

"Mr Jameson, please take your seat. From your own memories and those from the accused, we can see Ms Ashes has not manipulated anyone, does the jury agree?" All twelve heads nod, and the Judges question

"Mr Jameson, you will return to your cell. I don't believe ALL evidence was taken into account, so your original case will be reviewed," the judge bangs the gavel

"Court dismissed" Saint appears at my side, cutting off Jameson's view of me, and he takes me directly home; he has already filled in our family with everything that happened. I curl up in his arms and fall asleep.

When I wake, Dad is there.

"*Baby girl, I need to say sorry yet again, for failing you*" I go to speak, but he holds up his hand.

"No, let me finish, I am aware it's not fully my fault, you mentioned Jameson's stepfather at the trial" I give him a nod.

"I never met him, heard his and another man's voice over phone calls, but that doesn't help with identifying them. There is a note in one of the books I gave Dec when I first arrived" he gives me another nod.

"Well, let me fill in some of the blanks, but I'm going to keep it short-ish" Another nod from me, Ren puts an arm around me, and it's then I notice Dec, Saint, Bray and Grumps all sat here too.

"Your notes mentioned a guy with a southern accent," a slight nod from me as Dec crouches by me,

"Is this the voice?" he presses play on his voicemail.

"Ivanova, I didn't authorise you to move on Inferno or work with Demons"

Dec cuts the playback, and I nod. He moves to another message

"I've checked again and there are no records, whatever you smelt at the Pit was wrong"

I blink at them, and Saint fills in the gap.

"The first voice is a higher up, in our ranks, level with Mika, the second was his mate's other mate, and Jameson's stepdad, they both rejected their mate as she was human, but stayed friends" I give him a nod, but not sure how to react.

"When you and Saint left the pit, it was me who slammed your door open. He was telling me that there was only Saint in the room, and Saint always protected you." I look at Saint, and he mouths Sorry to me.

"Not your fault, I wouldn't have met Dan and Elise if you hadn't taken me to that hospital. I now know why Dec complained that you were always so close to finding me; it also explains how Jameson knew you were close and to move me. Any idea of their goal?" I ask taking the tea mug from Brayden.

"Yes, you were to replace their mates place, your blood showed you were strong, they hoped to break your will by putting you where you were over the years, they knew a lot more than what Jameson was aware of, we found plans that they were planning to take TripleMoon and due to your link to Liam his assets too, they knew you were with Dan and Elise but because of who Dan was they left you alone, not wanting to risk his wrath." my mouth drops open and Bray laughs.

"Yeah, they didn't have it all planned out; that's why they gave you to Lennox to get their help." We talk for a little longer, then I go in search of my children, needing to banish the bad with the amazing life I now have.

CHAPTER THIRTY-FIVE

KODIAK

I sit watching my angel sleep. Six days ago, we found out Samuel Jackson was murdered by another prisoner, who the next day confessed everything to his counsellor before reporting to his duties, climbing into a washing machine that auto washes when the door is shut. He was at a few places with Ember over the years, including The Tank, but he wasn't one of the lucky ones; he was serving time for killing his foster parents, who had been lacing his food with drugs, then filming his abuse to sell it. Ember petitioned to have his remains brought here, and he will be the first added to our memorial garden for fallen souls.

Rowan stirs in my arms. She was born by C-section five days ago. She takes after me in size and is closer to the size of a three-month-old than a five-day-old. After realising how big she was, Ember, Oriana and Xander all agreed it was safer not to have a natural birth.

My Angel got upset about the new Scar but none of us have ever found her repulsive 'her words not ours' and the new one is proof she brought our perfect daughter into this world, I love to lick the stretch marks on her beasts, thighs, ass, her tummy ones that I know more than just me spends time kissing each one, all of us that have yet to have a child with her have taken a six month injection to give her body time to heal, as soon as the C-section was decided we all agreed before she asked for time.

I hear our eldest coming along the hall, ready to change out of their school clothes, another of Embers amazing ideas, our kids are safe but still learning and in a structured environment, seven of the kids that have moved up to the high school that are at the pack group home have already asked Ren if they can join the pack when they graduate, they all have clear goals of what they want to do in life, so we started building some dorm type cabins, that will be situated on the drive.

Taylor Welsh, the Judge who oversaw Jameson's case against Ember, offered out his legal team to help any children that come through our schools, the hounds, the quad, Bas and Timber have all taken on a fair few as apprentices. We've even had some requests to transfer to our school to help smarter kids who are getting lost in the system. We have five who will graduate soon who have asked to join Saint and Dec's unit.

Things are actually looking good at the moment, since the Mating Ceremony, no one else has come forward trying to claim any of us away from Ember. We've had a few requests for arranged mating to our kids, but they were dismissed within seconds.

"Papa Kodi, can we come in?" a small voice whispers. I glance at Kota, whose head is poking through the door, and nod, all four filing in, kissing my cheek and Rowan's head before crawling on the bed to give their mother cuddles.

"Is mommy going to be okay?" Dante asks, looking worried.

"She will be fine, because Rowan was a bigger baby; it's just made mummy extra tired." I try to keep my voice soft, not wanting to wake her, but my Angel is already awake,

"I still love you all, though, always will," she vows to them,

"We know, Mommy, we're just worried," Dante says. They break into excited chatter about three new students at school, Dante asking if one of the girls can come live with us, and once they leave to do their homework, Ember is messaging Mickey G.

"Ren knew when we were four, so I'm not surprised," she smiles and takes Rowan to change her nappy while I get her bottle. Ember tried breastfeeding our Quads, but it was easier and nicer for us if we bottle-fed, so she never tried with any of the others.

When I reach the kitchen, I find Amelia baking sweet treats for the children for their snacks.

"Amelia, can you set up one of the empty rooms near Dante's? When you get a free minute? We may have a new member joining us." I send Miles a text to find out about clothes. When I get back upstairs with the bottle, Ren and Ember are on loudspeaker with Mickey G.

REN

I have no idea why. We know who Arya's mates are, and one of our unborn children is fated to the scary Demon trio, but this is more nerve-racking.

"As she is placed within our group home, it's a simple form to transfer to your full care, but I want to double-check, as eventually they will be teenagers." I chuckle at Mickey G's words. "Yeah, we're sure I never would have let Ember out of my sight if that bastard hadn't stolen her, and I think the urge to claim and breed would have been less if she had grown up with us. They will go on birth control as soon as they hit puberty, like all the kids in our care are." I kiss Ember's temple.

"Lia is sorting out a room, and I've texted Miles to sort out some clothes," Kodi states, passing Ember a bottle, then settling down on the other side of her.

"Persephone Winston, she is a year younger, so at least they will have a little separation, just be ready when she starts high school." he chuckles down the phone and confirms he will be over with paperwork tomorrow.

EMBER

I've been back to normal for three months now, and watching Ren sympathise with Dante has kept us all laughing. Effie is definitely sassy, a lot more than I ever was, to Miles' delight. Her favourite colour is pink, and she loves tutus, especially when combined with combat boots and skulls. Vicki also got excited by this, but we had to tell her that weapons as gifts were a sweet sixteen onwards, before that, not a good idea.

Black combat boots with a pink sole, striped black and pink tights with sparkly skull and crossbones, pink and grey tutu over black denim shorts with a long-sleeved t-shirt that says glitter is made from unicorn farts, and her cute little pixie haircut is the way she rolls most days. Effie is a nature mage. We've had to renovate her room as high emotions trigger her powers. When she woke from a bad dream two days after she moved in, Dante charged into her room to her screaming. She yelled at him when he was trying to see if she was okay.

"Don't care, stupid dream, you stomped my pretty flowers." So, then Dante was sent out while I hugged her crying body over flowers. Her entire floor was covered in wildflowers, some very rare, that Lia and Jake moved to the greenhouse. Dante had stomped straight to Kodi and Jake and asked if they could make pots and things for her pretty flowers, so he didn't get yelled at for stomping them again. We've added a Balcony to her room that was an enclosed open air Garden so she had plenty of space for her plants, because of the placement of her room, it means I have a flowered arch over one of my doors out of my studio, so we have added some seats and a table and its now where I sit for my lunch when working.

Just after my twenty-seventh birthday, I found out I was pregnant with baby number twelve, and by month two, we knew it was Tricks. He went full caveman and waited on me hand a foot; the guys wound him up constantly saying he had been body snatched. On Easter Sunday, which was three weeks earlier than we expected, I gave birth to Aimi-Rose our third little Kitsune of the pack, I get the irony my sweet tooth mate became a bio dad on a day filled with chocolate eggs, within moments Trick had her in a 'daddy's little girl' Harley Quinn baby grow, Arya had the traditional black and red diamond and Jester hat stuff so logically Aimi got the newer stuff, Forest had a few Joker things for when they were Kitsune'ing the latter normally the voice of reason but they already had a prank plan for when Aimi was older, Jenson was acting suspicious once and we found his office supplies where he had turned one of his bedside draws into a filing cabinet, he also has photo albums with before during and after photos.

CHAPTER THIRTY-SIX

EMBER

I missed Aimi's second Birthday as I was in the birthing room with Ren, so while the others blew out candles and played musical statues, Ren was passing me a gorgeous little girl, skin as white as marble and eyes a vivid ivy color, there was only one name for our little vampire, Ren passed Ivy over to Devin and I started to push again.

I screamed when three people appeared at the foot of the bed. Until it registered who they were, I yelled again.

> "DON'T FUCKING STAND THERE STARING
> AT MY VAGINA! SIT OVER THERE!"

I yelled and pointed to the couch, and with a final push, I felt the baby come into this world.

EVAN

I sucked in a breath as my heart stuttered a beat, our mate was being born, and the three of us went straight there. A scream put us on alert until we realised it was Ember yelling at us. A universal,
"Oh....ewww" went through us as we shuffled to the sofa when we realised we were staring at her painful-looking lady parts.
I remembered why I'm gay. Women are not pretty down there by any stretch of the imagination, especially when there is a four-inch round head being forced out of it, poor Ember.

CREED

I'd shot into the room at Ember's scream only to find her yelling at the not-so-scary Demon Trio. I laughed at the slightly green-kicked puppy look they all wore as they sat on the couch,

"I take it Felix decided to turn up for cuddles," I say, walking over to my tired mate, kissing her before I pick up my son, who's a wolf/incubus hybrid and also an omega. I knew his mates were desperate to meet him, but I also needed a few minutes. I was so scared for him and his future with them,

"We will keep him safe just like we do Miles, and those three will probably go on a rampage when he gets an owie from dropping one of his wooden blocks on his foot." Ren pats me on the shoulder I hear a few chuckles and hums, I walk over to Ishi and place my son in his arms, Evan places a soft kiss on the crown of Felix's head and Angel is running a finger over the top of his foot, an opal glow surrounds them, when it stops the three Demons have a mark around their ring fingers and so does Felix.

"There is a house for the three of you and Felix when he turns eighteen on the other side of the lake. The pack has been warned that when you are in residence, there will be more Demons around and probably a few guards for the baby." Ember's soft voice startles them

"Fank Ewe." Evan seems to be the only one who can speak; the others just smile. Ember starts pushing again, and soon I am passed a baby girl, unlike her Twin, she is an Alpha but still a hybrid,

"I think Luna and Dante are going to butt heads." Ember yawns, and soon we are setting down the babies. The Demons are going to check out their new home, letting us sleep.

CHAPTER THIRTY-SEVEN

EMBER

Fourteen days after Dante, Arya, Forest and Kota turn eighteen the whole pack celebrates Arya's mating to the Litter, she admitted to me she never liked any boys and around sixteen she realised why it was only ever Ryland, Cin and Ajax she saw a future with, but boy did she put them through hell, she and Miles have been planning the ceremony since her seventeenth when she told me and Ren she didn't want them to wait longer than they already had she knew they were her forever.

Her brothers always reassured the Litter that no one had tried more than talking to her, and knowing she was following her dad down the MMA route, they were more worried about others than her.

Thankfully, over the years, we've had very few problems outside the pack and the ones inside the pack were quickly sorted.

Ren has retired from professional fighting and now helps Brayden with training sessions at a gym they've opened in town. Saint and Declan left the force and finished opening their security firm with Silas and a few others from their unit. A lot of them got a kick out of Dad being below Dec in rank now.

Declan and Victoria now have five kids, Dec has also started rocking the silver fox look. Dad and Lily had another two kids, and Miles is pregnant with quads at the moment.

The amazing Omega owns a stylist company that does your home and wardrobe all in one, so between Saint and Dec's security, Bas and Timber building homes, Kodi doing custom furniture, The Quad doing the landscaping and Miles styling your décor and clothes, we are a one-stop family. Effie wants to combine part of Miles and The Quads business to do happy outdoors areas with plants that suit the person, so someone in a high stress job needs a calming area, she's also told Dante he needs to wait until she is twenty before they will be mating, we know they have started sleeping together 'shifter noses and all that' but Xander confirmed he had the talk with them both and they are on contraception.

JENSON

I don't have favourites, but Arya and I have always been close and seeing her take the next step in her life makes me realise how far we've come. Arya starts glancing around, then sighs, whispers something to Ajax, and then walks away. He watches her go with a soft smile.

When she reaches my biological daughter, I become concerned. None of us has ever shown favouritism to any of the kids, and some of us, like me with Arya, have bonded more with those not of our direct DNA; they all hold a piece of Ember, so we love them equally. I walk over when I notice more of the girls huddled around Aimi-Rose, she takes after me a lot, she has traditional Japanese features, long dark hair, she's quiet and reserved but she has a mischievous side 'careful of the quiet ones' rings true with her, she sits and watches and plots it took a while for us to realise some of the pranks were her.

I stand close but don't crowd, and slip my hands in my pockets.
"Aimi please talk to me," a young male voice says, I don't turn I just raise an eyebrow as I look Aimi in the eyes, at Aimi's nod I turn and find one of the guards the Demons have in place to protect our son, I tip my chin at him and with a sigh he follows I feel Evan step up next to me.

The young male looks between us, then hangs his head.
"I said something stupid and now she won't even talk to me," he mumbles, his head bowed even further.
"What?" Evan is always light on words, but somehow, he always gets the right tone, so more aren't needed.
"I asked why her hair was a silly colour, normally her hair is pretty black, with yellow and purple woven in underneath, but I saw she had a stormy grey instead, and it looked wrong. I wanted to know why she changed it, but she ran off." he looks close to tears.
"What's your name?" he glances at me, then looks back at the floor,

"Drake, Sir." I choke a little at the Sir but ignore it,

"Well, Drake, some Kitsunes show their emotions through their hair colour." he glances up with a frown, then gasps as I change mine,

"Yellow means she's happy, dark purple is playful or mischievous."

He's nodding, and I can see he's taking it all in. It feels odd to be the serious one.

"A stormy bluey grey means she's sad, find out why she was sad to begin with, then make it better, if you can't make it better, then tell me so I can find a way to make her smile. We guys always say the wrong thing, just means we become experts at saying sorry." He frowns for a bit, then smiles, asks Evan something in Latin, I know a few words, but I'm not fluent, finally he says thank you to us both and goes to head off,

"When you have some time off, my mate has a book on Kitsunes, have a read, it might explain some of our quirks. Most think they are stupid, but there is a reason for most things," he gives me another thank you, sir and walks away. My phone pings as I watch him doing something on his phone.

> **EVAN: He's asked me to get**
> **him some thread from our home,**
> **It's only made there.**
> **He thinks some girls at school are**
> **saying mean things, so he will let us**
> **know what he finds out.**

I smile and pat Evan's shoulder, then head to Quinny to let her know, but she already knows about the bullies and is working with the school to sort it. Once again, I bow to the awesomeness of my mate.

CHAPTER THIRTY-EIGHT

PAXTON

Harley and Bishop were born together and none of us were really shocked when we found out that they shared a mate, what left a bad taste in my mouth was it was the daughter of Shannon, one of the Barbies that tried to claim me as hers when Ember first arrived, it wasn't until a chance meeting with her, at the junk yard we regularly use that, as it turns out, her dad owns that I realised she was nothing like her mum, she rocked oil stained dungarees, and dirt smudged on her face. Harley practically swallowed his tongue when she walked in to apply for an apprenticeship with Linc doing tattoos, it took me a minute to recognise her, she was still in dungarees but they hugged her figure she had an AC/DC tank on underneath that fit her, it looked like one her dad had grown out of, so she brought it in her size, she had thick framed glasses on and she was also what my Pixie had been accused of being a human.

Ember found out she was the product of a one night stand and when Shannon found out she had no powers she dumped her with her dad, he was aware of us as there had been a few whoops moments with the Litter when they were little but he was fine with it, just angry at Shannon who, by all accounts, was a shit lay.

Ember soon took Sapphire, or Saf as she prefers, under her wing. They bonded over art, and once Ember had soothed those 'you're not a worthless human' booboos, she was around ours for dinner with paint smudged on her face, with Ember regularly. The boys asked us about getting a cabin built for them, now she's still sporting the dungarees but she also has a cute little baby bump, with our first grandchild growing, I try not to stare while we wait for Aimi to walk down the aisle, Effie has covered the floor in Japanese wild flowers, including some in pots near the alter from the demon realm. I glance at the blessing arch adorned with a rainbow of lilies and watch as a very nervous Drake flickers between his demon and human form, Ryuu is at his side to calm him, he partially shifts so his wings are visible so are his horns and tail, little puffs of smoke coming from his nose, all nerves are forgotten when Aimi appears between Ember and Jenson, wearing one of J's moms traditional Kimonos her hair flickering through a rainbow of colours before their eyes meet and it settles on yellow.

EMBER

Holding our first Grandchild is daunting. I'm not even 40 yet, and somehow the baby girl holds both her daddies, types Basilisk/Nightmare hybrid. I pass Indigo back to her mother before bidding her good night. In a few weeks, it's Luna and Felix's turn to be mated. It was Felix's idea to have a joint ceremony, and the biggest Diva was, of course, Angel. Thankfully, Felix has kept him reined in; they are the final two of my born babies to be mated. When the youngest turned 16, we started fostering, and like Uncle Nic, some chose to stay, and our packs have continued to grow.

Liam finally moved into his own home that borders onto TripleMoon and BloodMoon packlands. After a few months, he got bored and decided to renovate it into an Arts school for the supernatural. He covers all types of art, including music, and I do the odd workshop for him now and then.

CHAPTER THIRTY-NINE

TRENT

I watch as Felix has a blessing from one of the Princes of Hell before the Prince returns to his own realm, and then it's Luna's turn to walk down the aisle, who would have thought that me, a lynx shifter, would be standing here ready to be blessed to my Alpha and Luna's youngest daughter, and an Alpha female at that.

I was fine to begin with, Luna was just another of Ember's amazing kids, until she hit puberty, then I became a giggling mess, blushing each time, she looked in my direction. Now, the twenty-one-year-old female with a partial doctorate in psychology is walking towards me.

"Breath Trent" I hear Ren whisper behind me and I take a huge breath, Luna takes my hand and then she guides me through our blessing, I can't stop looking at her, everything but her is a blur, until we reach the door to my cabin, as she closes the door, I pull her into my lap on the sofa.

"I have a confession", I look down at our linked hands,

"You were my first kiss, Luna. I have no experience. I never wanted anything from anyone until you," she presses her lips to mine.

"Take me to bed, Trent, let's learn together." I take a deep breath

"Trust me?" she whispers into my chest.

"Always."

CHAPTER FOURTY

EMBER

All my life, or for at least as long as I can remember, two wolves visit me in my dreams or save me from my bad dreams, they are the one good constant in my life.......... Or they were I now have three loving grandfathers, a dad who has a super-hot mate, two doting uncles, four brothers and three sisters, a huge amount of nieces, nephews and some non-blood related cousins, ten mates, fifteen amazing biological children and I've lost count how many grandkids and great grandkids I have!

Not bad for a broken shifter.

Remember you are worth the price you give yourself, doesn't matter how different you are from your parents, siblings or those in your town.

If you want the stars, you raise your chin and work hard; you will eventually reach them. Be the Phoenix and rise from the ashes, then howl at the moon, when you reach the stars.

When Embers become Ashes
A Phoenix will Rise
And the Wolves will Howl at the Bloodmoon

EPILOGUE

MAKAYL

It's been ten years since we lost my dad, twelve since we lost Trunk and fifteen since Pops left us, only five since we lost Alma, and now Nic, Luc and I are sitting in rocking chairs watching the Great-Great Grandkids find their mates, our first Great-Great-Great is on the way. Liam finally found his mate, who happened to be one of Felix's Babies. Nate found two in Luna's set of Twins. Luc met his human mate in town when she tripped and took out Amelia's bedding stall a few months ago, and is planning to bring her into the know of the supernatural. She grew up in care but was a lucky one and owns her own business making jams and pickles.

Makes you wonder if I hadn't had that one-night stand, if Ember hadn't survived and made it to us, a lot of people could have missed out on a lot of happiness. Everything happens for a reason, and just like my daughter has, life is what you make it; it just takes work, no matter where you start out. A Phoenix will always be born from Ashes.

PACK
MEETING
HOUSE

TRIPLEMOON
PACK

LIAM'S ESTATE

SCHOOL

GROUNDS
KEEPER

DORMS

GYM

CINEMA

XANDER'S

MILL

ATELIER

BLOODMOON

BARN

DRUGSTORE

OPERA

LIBRARY

SAW
MILL

XANDER'S
CLINIC

TREHI
LARES

CALLUM
MARCUS

KODI
SHOWROOM

TimeLine

BIRTH: 31ST DECEMBER

GROUP HOME

4 YEARS OLD

BLOODWOLF PACK 14TH MARCH

6 YEARS OLD

HELLBLOOD MOTORCYCLE CLUB 3RD JANUARY

7 YEARS OLD

GROUP HOME 12TH JANUARY
TWIN TREES PACK 2ND FEBUARY
GROUP HOME 18TH APRIL
THE DEN 1ST MAY
GROUP HOME 25TH DECEMBER

8 YEARS OLD

SHARPE FAMILY 10TH JAUARY
CLAWFANG PACK 15TH MAY
GROUP HOME 6TH AUGUST
LANE FAMILY 23RD NOVEMBER

9 YEARS OLD

ARMATIGE FAMILY 22ND JANUARY
GROUP HOME 17TH APRIL
TRACY FAMILY 27TH APRIL
QUADRIVER PACK 6TH JULY
JACOBEY FAMILY 10TH OCTOBER
LAKEVIEW PACK 6TH NOVEMBER

10 YEARS OLD

THE TANK 4TH FEBUARY
GROUP HOME 1ST DECEMBER
THE CAGE 17TH DECEMBER

11 YEARS OLD

GROUP HOME 3RD SEPTEMBER
HOSPITAL 15TH SEPTEMBER
THE PIT 17TH SEPTEMBER

12 YEARS OLD,
13 YEARS OLD

HOSPITAL 1ST JULY
SHIELD FAMILY 8TH JULY

14 YEARS OLD
15 YEARS OLD

HALFWAY HOUSE 1ST AUGUST

16 YEARS OLD

LENNOX PACK 4TH NOVEMBER
HOSPITAL MID DECEMBER 2018

17 YEARS OLD

TRIPLE MOON PACK 21ST JANUARY

18 YEARS OLD

BLOODMOON PACK 31ST DECEMBER

WHO IS WHO

TRIPLEMOON BABIES

LUKA NATHANIEL - WOLF
NIKITA BUNICA - WOLF/SUCCUBI HYBRID

BLOODMOON BABY MATES

DRAKE - DEMON
SAPHIRE - HUMAN
PERSEPHONE WINSTON/EFFIE - EARTH MAGE

EMBER'S BABIES

KOTA - WOLF/MAGE HYBRID
FOREST - WOLF/KITSUNE - DUEL SHIFTER
ARYA - KITSUNE
DANTE - ALPHA WOLF
AIMI-ROSE - KITSUNE
BISHOP - NIGHTMARE
MELODY - NIGHTMARE
FELIX - OMEGA INCUBI/WOLF HYBRID
LUNA - ALPHA WOLF/SUCCUBI HYBRID
MIA - WOLF/SUCCUBI HYBRID
LEXIE - WOLF/SUCCUBI HYBRID
HARLEY - BASILISK
ROWAN - ALASKAN MOUNTAIN BEAR
IVY - VAMPIE
RYUU - DRAGON

BLOODMOON BABIES

LACEY - WOLF
BRONWEN - BLOOD DRAGON
REYNA - CRYSTAL MAGE
HUGO
RAVEN WILLOW - EARTH MAGE/WOLF HYBRID
PHOENIX OAKLY - EARTH MAGE/WOLF HYBRID
INDIGO - NIGHTMARE/BASILISK HYBRID
HELENA - LYNX
ALEXANDER - LYNX/INCUBI HYBRID
NOEL - DEMON/INCUBI HYBRID

WHO IS WHO

ELDERS COUNCIL

DEMON REPRESENTATIVE - VICTORIA
VAMPIRE REPRESENTATIVE - WOLFGANG
SUCCUBI REPRESENTATIVE - BECKY
INCUBI REPRESENTATIVE - DAMON
DRAGON REPRESENTATIVE - RHETT
MAGE REPRESENTATIVE - BLAIR - ORACLE
NIGHTMARE REPRESENTATIVE - ENOX
PREY SHIFTER REPRESENTATIVE - COLIN - ROBIN
HELLHOUND REPRESENTATIVE - DANIEL
PREDATOR SHIFTER REPRESENTATIVE - JESSICA - POLAR BEAR
ANGEL REPRESENTATIVE - MADAM CELEST

FAMILY MEMBERS

MIKHAL IVANOVA - EMBER'S FATHER - ALPHA WOLF
DOMINIC IVANOVA - TRIPLEMOON ALPHA, EMBER'S UNCLE - ALPHA WOLF
LUCIAN IVANOVA - TRIPLEMOON BETA, EMBER'S UNCLE - BETA WOLF
NIKOLAI IVANOVA - EMBER'S GRANDFATHER - ALPHA WOLF
DECLAN TREEFALL - TRIPLEMOON'S FUTURE ALPHA, EMBER'S HALF BROTHER - VAMPIRE
BASTILLE TREEFALL - EMBER'S HALF BROTHER - ALASKAN MOUNTAIN BEAR
BRAEDEN FENRIS IVANOVA - EMBER'S TWIN BROTHER - DUAL BETA WOLF

MILES - OMEGA ALBINO PANTHER - BRAYDEN'S MATE
BRANLEY STOKES - DRAGON/VAMPIRE HYBRID - MILES AND MATTEO'S MATE
MATTEO MICHAELS - CRYSTAL MAGE - MILES AND BRANLEY'S MATE

LILLIANA VOLKOV - SEELCHEN - MOYRAG'S MATE
PRINCE LIAM GIDEONSON - VAMPIRE PRINCE
SIR NATHANIEL PRINCE - VAMPIRE - ROYAL GUARD

ALMA GERRY - ELEMENTAL MAGE - TRIPLEMOON HOUSEKEEPER

TRUNK TREEFALL - ALASKAN MOUNTAIN BEAR, KODIAK'S GRANDFATHER, BASTILLE'S UNCLE
TIMBER TREEFALL - ALASKAN MOUNTAIN BEAR - KODIAK'S OLDER BROTHER

XANDER FIREFALL - BETA WOLF - REX AND JENSON'S OLDER HALF - BROTHER

EMBERS MATES

REN FIREFALL - ALPHA WOLF
JENSON FALL - KITSUNE
CREED TATE - INCUBUS/WOLF HYBRID
JACE TATE - WOLF/INCUBUS HYBRID
KODIAK TREEFALL - ALASKAN MOUNTAIN BEAR
DARBY O'CONNERS - DRAGON
DEVIN MOORE - VAMPIRE
SAINT KNIGHT - NIGHTMARE
RIVER KNIGHT - NIGHTMARE
PAXTON STONE - BASILISK

182

WHO IS WHO

FAMILY MEMBERS

Mayhal Ivanov - Ember's Father - Alpha Wolf
Dominic Ivanov - TripleMoon Alpha, Ember's Uncle - Alpha Wolf
Lucian Ivanov - TripleMoon Beta, Ember's Uncle - Beta Wolf
Argo Ivanov - Ember's Grandfather - Alpha Wolf
Declan Ivanov - TripleMoon's Future Alpha, Ember's Half Brother - Vampire
Bastille TreeFall - Ember's Half Brother - Alaskan Mountain Bear
Braiden Evans Ivanov - Ember's Twin Brother - Dual Beta Wolf

Miles - Omega Albino Panther - Braidey's Mate
Bradley Stokes - Dragon/Vampire Hybrid - Miles and Matteo's Mate
Matteo Michaels - Crystal Mage - Miles and Bramdly's Mate

Lillian Volkov - Sleteckis - Mayhal's Mate
Prince Liam Giovonson - Vampire Prince
Sir Nathaniel Prince - Vampire - Royal Guard

Aima Guidry - Elemental Mage - TripleMoon Housekeeper

Trunk TreeFall - Alaskan Mountain Bear, Kodiak's Grandmother, Bastille's Uncle
Timber TreeFall - Alaskan Mountain Bear - Kodiak's Older Brother

Vander FreeFall - Beta Wold - Ren and Jenson's Older Half Brother

EMBERS MATES

Ren FreeFall - Alpha Wolf
Jenson Fall - Kitsune
Creed Tate - Incubus/Wolf Hybrid
Jace Tate - Wolf/Incubus Hybrid
Kodiak TreeFall - Alaskan Mountain Bear
Darby O'Conners - Dragon
Devin Moore - Vampire
Saint Knight - Nightmare
River Knight - Nightmare
Payton Stone - Basilisk

OTHER MAIN CHARACTERS

Giovanni Michaels - Vampire - Social Worker
Ignatious Salvator - Dragon - Lawyer

HELLHOUNDS

Pops - Reginald
Nonna - Passed
Layton
Deeon
Bear
Rachet
Silas
Link
Ryland, Ajax, Cin (The Litter)

RELUCTANTLY ADDED

Samual Jameson - Social Worker - Mage

THE TREEFALL FAMILY TREE

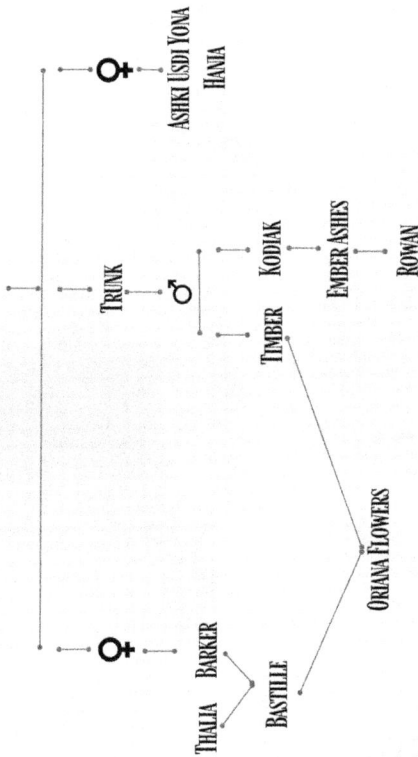

TreeFall Senior — Mama TreeFall

♀ Ashki Usdi Yona · Hania

♂ Trunk
- Kodiak — Ember Ashes — Rowan
- Timber — Oriana Flowers

♀ Thalia · Barker
- Bastille — Oriana Flowers

THE BLOODMOON FAMILY TREE

EMBER ASHES

SAINT KNIGHT — BISHOP

PAXTON STONE — HARLEY — SAPHIRE, INDIGO

REN FIREFALL
- KOTA — FOREST
- DANTE — ARYA — RYLAND, CIN
- AIMI-ROSE — PERSEPHONE WILSON — AJAX

JENSON FALL — DRAKE

KODIAK TREEFALL — ROWAN

RIVER KNIGHT — MELODY

CREED TATE
- FELIX — ANGEL, EVAN, HELENA, ISHILDUR — NOEL, LIAM ♂ ♀ ♂ ♀ ♂
- LUNA — TRENT — ALEXANDE, NATE

JACE TATE — MIA — LEXIE

DARBY O'CONNERS — RYUU

DEVIN MOORE — IVY

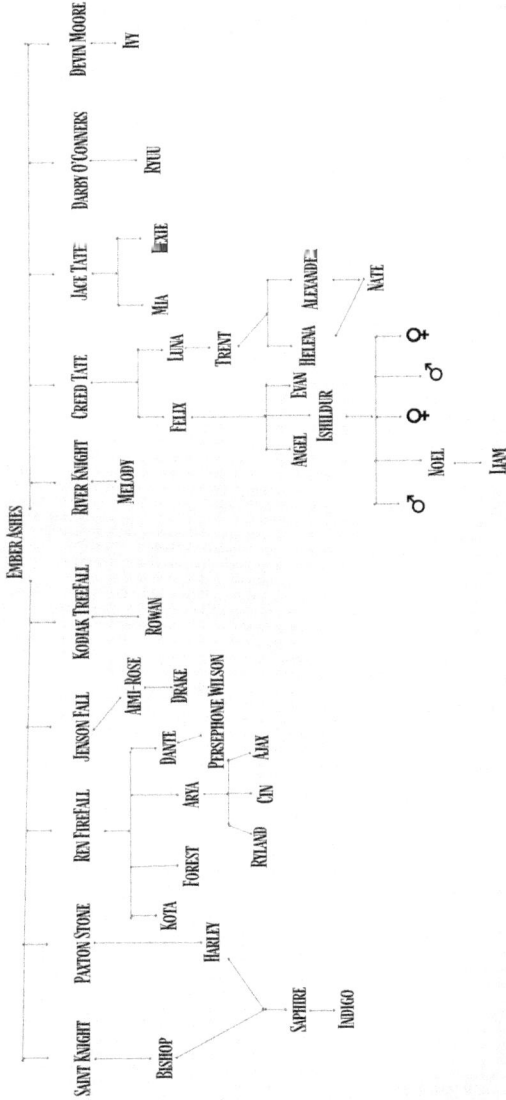

185

THE TRIPLEMOON FAMILY TREE

NIKOLI IVANOVA — BUNICA IVANOVA

LUCIAN
HUMAN FEMALE NEVER NAMED

DOMANIC
PASSED AWAY AT A YOUNG AGE

MAKYAL — LILIANA VOLKOV

♀

♂

NIKITA

LUKA

THALIA

EMBER

BRAYDEN

BASTILLE

TREFALL

ORIANA

?

DECLAN

VICTORIA

♀
♂
♀
♀

MILES

BRAYDEN

BRAMLEY — MATTEO

LACEY

BRONWEN

REYNA

AUTHOR NOTE

There have been tears, tantrums and a lot of foul language.
BookWifey is ready to divorce me, from the
random questions over the last three plus years,
but the cliff-hangers are all her fault.

FYI – we are not married, we are just friends, our sons have been
friends for six years, and we have known each other for over ten.

This was my first, and it always will hold a special
place in my heart. And I know there are some parts
that you want more of, and you want more from some
of the other characters, and those may happen in the
future, but right now, I need something new.

Hope you enjoy what comes next

x MercyAshes x

BOOKS IN THIS SERIES

The Bloodmoon trilogy

When Embers Become Ashes

A Phoenix Will Rise

And The Wolves Will Howl At The Bloodmoon

Miles Omega

MMMM Novella That Takes Place During Chapter Eight Of A Phoenix Will Rise

The Bloodmoon Anthology

Contains The Main Three Books and The Novella Miles Omega

BOOKS BY THIS AUTHOR

Lineout

Contemporary Reverse Harem Rugby Romance.

The Forbidden Obsession

Book One In The Velvet Mafia Novella Series.
M/F Contemporary Romance.

The Wedding

Book Two In The Velvet Mafia Novella Series.
M/F Contemporary Romance.

The First Kill

Book Three In The Velvet Mafia Novella Series.
M/F Contemporary Romance.

The Princess Of Hell's Fightclub

Paranormal Reverse Harem Standalone.